GOAT TREES

Tales from the Other Side of the World

GOAT TREES

Tales from the Other Side of the World

David Rozgonyi

WOLVERINE FARM
PUBLISHING

FORT COLLINS, CO

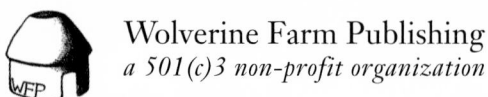

Wolverine Farm Publishing
a 501(c)3 non-profit organization

For information, address Wolverine Farm Publishing, P.O. Box 814, Fort Collins, Colorado 80522.

www.wolverinefarmpublishing.org
www.davidrozgonyi.com

Author photograph by Barbara Szigeti. All other photographs by the author.

FIRST EDITION
10 9 8 7 6 5 4 3 2 1

Manufactured in the United States of America on recycled paper according to industry standards established by the Green Press Initiative.

ISBN 0-9741999-6-6

For Alice,
to whom I dedicate
everything I've ever written
and everything I ever will.
I will always follow wherever you go;
I will always return to wherever you are.

Contents

A Cambodian Tale, Part I
(3 Years, 8 Months, 20 Days)
13

Snails of the South Pacific
47

Traveling on Trains
65

The Lion of Fez
87

Lightning
113

Goat Trees
131

An Autumn Scent
149

Love Among the Ruins
165

Interlude
175

Exhaust
187

A Cambodian Tale, Part II
(The Sunflower)
211

"I long to sleep in the cool, deep silence beneath the dizzying volley of stars, with nothing but the sky's infinite expanse for a roof and the warm earth for a bed . . . in the sorrowful yet serene knowledge that I am utterly alone, that no one pines for me anywhere on earth, that there is no place where I am being missed or expected. . . where I shall never be anything but an outsider, a stranger."

"The act of leaving is the bravest and most beautiful of all."

—Isabelle Eberhardt
b. 1877, Geneva—d. 1904, Aïn Sefra, Algeria
from *The Nomad: The Diaries of Isabelle Eberhardt*

A Cambodian Tale, Part I
(3 Years, 8 Months, 20 Days)

Not long before dark, a man wearing a high-collared shirt and brown slacks emerged from the corridors of a disused building in southern Phnom Penh. He crossed the flat expanse of ground that separated the gray three-story structure from its enclosure of featureless walls with long strides, each step coming a little more quickly than the one before. Moving fast, he glanced neither at the fourteen dwarfish tombs beneath the scraggly palms on his right, nor at the faces of the Khmers working to repair a broken drainpipe to his left. The gates ahead had fallen against each other during the half-hour he'd spent within, and now, tangled as they were with rusting razor wire, offered only a sliver of escape.

The lights in the hot city beyond them were just coming on, flickering fluorescents high on lampposts scattered like punctuation rather than as sources of illumination, and the shadows of creepers and vines tangled purely black among the weeds sprouting from every crack in the shattered concrete walk.

A report boomed, and the man's foot caught on a root that snaked through the dust across his way; the staccato rattle of backfire from a truck idling in one of the alleys startled him. Sweat stung his eyes, but then he was turning sideways, slipping through the gate, wincing as his shirt snagged on a shard of metal. He cursed a woman's name, the cotton ripped, and in the time it took to beg her forgiveness in his head, he was out.

Beyond the gates, the man entered a domain of rubble, haphazard structures falling down into entropic piles of brick and corrugated iron. Open sewage canals cut the warren of shacks in a Venetian parody along whose steeply pitched sides children fished with twigs. Coming into the long dry season, a rime of fine powder filled every glance, and reddened the sky, the backs of stray dogs, and the hundred faces that surrounded him the instant he left the protection of Toul Sleng behind.

They came at him in undershirts and balanced on crutches, holding baseball caps in their brown hands and wheedling. Clad in camouflage pants pinned high to resemble a large, full diaper, a shadow crawled forward on three stumps and a left arm. The voices were raised and coarse and the man laughed uncomfortably as he broke through their ranks—they couldn't move very fast with such mangled appendages—but immediately another, more mobile knot of motodrivers and tuk-tuk captains took over, cajoling, teasing. Maybe it was the light, red and failing, but all of them looked darker, more indigenous, than he remembered the Khmers to be only a few hours north of here. That had been a respite, a fortuitous first stop on a quest of many stops; this alley rudely pinched between rusting buildings and endless barbed wire was a frontier.

The man tightened his lips and pushed toward his destination—a diminutive wooden guesthouse, the only welcoming place for miles and where he'd left his suitcase. Although it was only ten meters across the alley, it might have been a thousand, a vast plain populated by waving brown fingers and shirts flapping from skeletal bodies like rags caught in bare trees. Someone touched his back, a hand was on his arm, a rush of fetid breath against his face, but then he lunged past the potted plants that guarded the entrance of the guesthouse, heart-shaped leaves brushed his head like a mother's hand, and the beggars and the drivers were gone.

The silence was immediate, though not total—a plunge under water and then a surface for breath. The narrow murk of the courtyard was cluttered with bamboo tables at which several young couples in gauzy shirts sat drinking beer and leaning against walls, the backs of the rickety chairs, each other. Their breaths were rapid and shallow, their faces shiny with sweat, visibly exhausted as though they had run the breadth of the city to arrive here only moments before, when in reality they, too, had only just stumbled in from across the way.

The man slipped between the tables and through a myriad of potted tropical plants as thick as any jungle, broke through blue filigrees of incense, to the back, where the young man who ran the restaurant and the four rooms upstairs stood waiting. A small kitchen whose ceiling towered above it to encompass the second floor of the guesthouse clanked and bustled behind him.

"Okay, Mr. Nong, I'll take the room, but only if it has an attached bath," he told the young proprietor. It was the only possible conclusion to the conversation started an hour ago when he'd dropped off his suitcase. "Air-conditioning, too," he added. "I'll die without the air."

"Very good. I'm Mr. N'gon. What is your name?"

"Jack."

"You are very lucky, Jack. Our best room is empty. It is too expensive for our regular customers." He smiled—big, healthy white teeth in two beautiful rows, Jack noted—and thumbed a page of his cracked ledger to make a note of his own. "Only for special guests. How did you find the attraction?"

"The old high school across the street, the boneyard or whatever the hell it is? *Toul Sleng*? I wasn't in the mood for that at all, to tell you the truth. I'm a little sorry you suggested it. But it wasn't as bad as I thought it would be. If you painted it something other than gray, it wouldn't look out of place here, really." Jack laughed and pointed behind him, then realized that he was indicting the very house in which he now stood, and his arm dropped back to his side. "A couple thousand yearbook photos, splatters on the ceiling here and there, a few bloodstains on the floors." Jack licked his lips and tented the front of his shirt, circulating musky air. "It's been twenty years—you really could clean it up a bit."

Mr. N'gon finished with the ledger, closed it and slid Jack his key. "It is what tourists come to see in *P'nm Pay-nh*. Perhaps tomorrow you can enjoy *Choeng Ek*. It is where the people in the yearbook photos were buried."

Jack held his hands out and shook his head. "Mr. Nong, I'm not a tourist, and I'm not here out of choice at all."

Lined with paper lamps and dark, old wood weathered by a half century of service, the upstairs landing was a small, square cube of gloom that served as an atrium for the four rooms that gave onto it. The floor bent alarmingly beneath his feet as Jack padded to his door, and when he got there, he realized that he could make out the tables below between the thin slats of the floorboards. He shook his head and slipped inside his room.

The whine of mosquitoes came from dark corners as he fumbled a cord for some light. He took a few steps toward the door that led to the bathroom, a step toward the window, a step toward a bed that perched like a spider on its tall, curved legs. There was no net above the bed, but that was okay. He wouldn't be opening the windows tonight, and the can of aerosol insect spray on the nightstand would make quick work of the bugs already inside. He used it, aiming a prolonged burst beneath a bed, then behind it, in all the corners and along all cracks in the cinder wall of the bathroom. He stood on the toilet and sprayed atop the scalding boiler, then stood on the green rattan futon beneath the long window above the kitchen, and sprayed the top of the curtain rod as well. He then sprayed beneath the futon, and between the curtain and the window, until an unexpected spasm of coughing forced him to stop.

The air-conditioner was mounted to the wall above the bed, and Jack stepped onto the hard mattress and examined it. Holding his breath, he pushed a button. The slender machine roared to life. The tails of his shirt began to flutter, and his sweaty hair began to dry.

Soon, mosquitoes began to fall out of the air, and after a deep, icy breath, he stepped down from the bed and meandered around the room, peering into the corners and nodding at the tangles of stiff little corpses there. Satisfied that nothing would come to disturb his rest, he pulled off his clothes, lowered himself onto his stomach, and dozed naked in the stream, cold and wonderful, that came from the air conditioner above his bed.

Brother, wake up!

Who is there? Brother? It is still dark—what is the matter?

Nothing, Brother. Work detail has changed.

Angkar needs you to cut rattan in Chamkar Chek. Get dressed.

> *That is several days away. Let me eat first for the journey.*

> *There is no need for that, Brother. We have plenty of rice. Hurry now!*

> *I must tell my wife and daughter I am leaving.*

> *There is no need. You will be back before your wife knows you're gone.*

Jack awakened with a stifled sound in his throat. He didn't know what had disturbed his sleep, but it quickly became apparent by the sound of cries from downstairs that something had changed. He opened his eyes wide, but the room was darker than seemed possible through the mere absence of light; there was a black hand over his eyes, over his nose, on his chest, in his gut. Jack rolled to the edge of the bed and knocked his forehead on the window glass; the kitchen below had no light either. But there were people in that darkness, slight forms scurrying back and forth. A circle of blue flared along a wall, soon joined by another beside it—the gas burners of the stoves. Bare feet slapped across tiles and from room to room, the stairs were groaning now beneath new weight, slats creaked, and then a girl in an adjacent room called out something unintelligible, her voice shrill. The sliver of space around the doorframe flickered as burning candles rushed about in the darkness.

Jack's heart slowed as he lay back on the mattress and blew out his cheeks. It was a power outage. Nothing more.

Recalling the general area of the room where he'd thrown his case, Jack crawled from the bed and swept around the floor until he bumped it with his hands. The flashlight was in the topmost pocket. Its thin cone of halogen blinded him.

For the moment, the air in the room was cold, so Jack satisfied himself to watch the activity below his window. Ten minutes passed. A wok began to toss through the murk, the flames of the stove leaping beneath its light-shadow. Another ten minutes passed. With a sigh, Jack slipped back into his musty clothes and descended the steep wooden stairs into the dark garden below.

There were more guests than before, twelve in all, and Mr. N'gon strolled between them with the Buddha's gentle smile.

Jack blocked his way. "My room has no power."

Mr. N'gon slipped easily past Jack's bulk without so much as brushing against him.

"It comes and goes. Maybe soon it will come. Perhaps you will enjoy a beer with us here."

Jack glanced around the garden. The exhausted people were still there, but their ranks had been diluted by less fragile newcomers—Toul Sleng closed at nightfall, so these guests had come only for the food. Candles burned on the tables and between the shrubs, beside the pots of palms and from sconces hanging from the eaves and the rafters, their flames perfect orange tulips. Four young men were playing cards; behind Jack, two girls were snickering softly over a book they shared.

Jack leaned toward Mr. N'gon so he could lower his voice. "My air conditioner is dead."

He needn't have bothered with discretion, because Mr. N'gon's voice cut cheerfully through the greenery. "None of the other rooms have air conditioning."

A moment later he vanished into the flickering kitchen and Jack returned to his room when he realized that it was still a few degrees cooler there than suffocating in this stifling and dark garden, listening to people his daughter's age laugh and whisper.

Why have we stopped?

Get out of the truck, Brother.

I would like to know! I was told we were going to harvest rattan!

Brother Cheang, blindfold this reactionary and strap his elbows together behind his back. Hurry now, do as I say.

Brother Serak, I have done nothing!

You are on the District Chief's list. Therefore you have been implicated in a plot to destroy Angkar. That is more than you deserve to know. Do not deny it or it will be worse.

But you must listen, I did nothing wrong. You have known me for five years! I am loyal to Angkar!

Brother Cheang, put his ankles in shackles. Tighten them down with the wrench. If he cries out, or speaks again, break his jaw.

The room grew rapidly hotter. Even with the air conditioning off for only twenty minutes, pearls of moisture clustered among the bristles on Jack's face and put the taste of salt on his tongue; those that dripped down his back felt like mosquitoes tickling his skin.

He lay down, but it was no better to be horizontal. The ceiling rose above him in a starless infinity as the bed sheets grew damp, then moist, then wet. He took to shifting positions every few minutes to cool himself. From downstairs, flames flared in the kitchen as the cooks lit more candles and started up another two gas burners. The odors of frying garlic and shrimp paste suffused the room and seemed to settle in his stomach; the heat from the kitchen transpired through the floor and turned the wood warm beneath his soles. When he could take no more, Jack went downstairs to again seek out Mr. N'gon, whom he found carefully lighting rods of yellow incense and setting them in pots of sand.

"Really, Mr. Nong, when might this be resolved so I can get a little rest?" Jack coughed. The sandalwood smoke was unfamiliar in his nose.

Mr. N'gon had the heavy eyes and soft, round mouth of a somnambulist. "This part of *P'nm Pay-nh* not have much electricity. Everyone want see Toul Sleng, but no one want stay here."

"I'm here! And they're here—" he pointed at a young couple. They looked startled by this, as though they only just realized they had no idea where they were. "We don't count for anything?" Jack cast an entreating glance around, but instead of sympathizers, he saw the front gate yawning hot breath into the garden. Shadows slipped through the gravel outside, receding and advancing, receding and advancing. "Don't you ever lock that?"

"But Mr. Jack, there is nothing to fear."

Jack shook his head. "The lights never go out in Siem Reap."

Up in Room 1, the air was a bath of heat, and the stench of food was overpowering. Jack threw open the glass—insects be damned—and the tiniest cooling breeze touched his sweaty face. Immediately, something bit him on the neck. He slapped at it and his hand came away bloodied. Instantly, another mosquito landed on his wrist, and dug in before he could dispatch it away. He cursed. The incense must have kept them away in the garden, but up here, they were thick and very fast. The other rooms all had screens on the doors and mosquito nets billowing over the beds, but not his, not this suite that cost twice as much as the rest. Jack closed the window and sat in the dark, refusing to let his mind run down the thin jungle paths there.

Read the sign carefully, Brother. I cannot say your life depends on it, for it is nearly over, but what is left might be a little easier.

1. *You must answer accordingly to my questions—don't turn them away.*

2. *Don't try to hide the facts by making pretexts this and that. You are strictly prohibited to contest me.*

3. *Don't be a fool for you are a chap who dared to thwart the revolution.*

4. *You must immediately answer my questions without wasting time to reflect.*

5. *Don't tell me either about your immoralities or the essence of the revolution.*

6. *While getting lashes or electrification you must not cry at all.*

7. *Do nothing, sit still and wait for my orders. If there is no order, keep quiet.*

8. *Don't make pretexts about Kampuchea Krom in order to hide your jaw of traitor.*

9. *If you don't follow all the above rules, you will get many lashes of electric wire.*

"I need a beer."

"Of course." Mr. N'gon disappeared into the kitchen and reappeared an instant later with a tall bottle of Kleang. Jack studied the elephant on the label as closely as if it were a vintage wine, and then set it down. "You don't have Angkor?"

"Maybe near temples . . . Here we have only Kleang."

"Then I guess it'll do."

During the hour Jack had spent upstairs,

tossing in a fitful place somewhere between sleep and unconsciousness, the garden had slowly emptied, and now only a few couples remained. Even these had the distant smiles of people about to rise to their feet and pick unsteady lines between the tables, some heading for the front gates, others for the stairs leading to their own dark rooms.

Jack took a wicker chair beneath the overhang of the guesthouse eaves and sipped his beer. Voices began to resolve out of the tangled shrubbery that surrounded him on three sides, and soon, he was able to make out the disembodied voices of a pair of British men.

"What a place, that," one of them said, as Jack stared at the elephant on the label of the beer. He didn't dare glance past the plants at the entrance, past the motos and the murk, for fear of catching a little of the deeper darkness that began at the gate across the alley.

"All of them are free men—that's what knackers me. The guards averaged what, fifteen years old? Fifteen plus twenty is only thirty-five. They're all still around, aren't they. Our drivers. Our cooks."

"The police, soldiers on the street corners."

"Smiley-chap over there." The man

pointed at Mr. N'gon, who waved cheerfully but made no move to approach. "*Yeah, hi there, big guy.* He could have been doling out 'many lashes of electric wire' for God's sake. How can he wake up every morning after that? How can he go and be a person?"

Jack wiped his mouth with the back of his hand and spoke to the shrubbery. "Because he's not old enough."

Silence, and then the leaves rustled. "How'dya know that, mate?"

"Teeth don't stay that perfect in a place like this for very long."

One of them blew air in disbelief, a watery noise like a porpoise broaching, and then their voices grew soft and repetitive. Jack finished his beer and hazarded a glance at the entrance. There were faces between the fat leaves, bony Khmer faces peering into the garden from the dirt alley outside. A one-legged man hopped forward, a dirty mother tried to smile, and Jack stood and returned to his room.

Before he could enter it, a woman's voice called out from the darkness.

"I've got a fan."

Jack assumed the voice had come from one of the other rooms, but in their uniformity—a ring of slatted, dark doors—he couldn't be sure which one contained her, let alone if the entreaty had been meant for him.

He cleared his throat. "There's no power. How can you have a fan?"

"Come on, I'll show you."

Her voice was familiar in its upturning amusement, a twenty-something on the verge of laughter, and Jack faced the gloom wide-eyed. At first there were only sparks at the corners of his vision, and he thought for an instant that the girl was having fun at his expense, but as he neared the middle of the square space, he heard a door grate open. He couldn't see which one.

"Hurry, or the mozzies'll eat us both up!"

Jack followed her voice into a room that was much smaller than his own, just a bed on the floor beneath a billowing white mosquito net and a black window thrown open to the night. The air was cool as it sighed through the opening, and carried with it not the smells of burnt garlic, but the fragrances of flowers.

The angular form beneath the white shroud spoke again. "Close that would you?"

Jack slid the door closed. Only then did the net shiver, then an edge rose up, and Jack crawled beneath like a boy hiding beneath his mother's skirt.

A girl sat cross-legged on the mattress, grinning at him in a smug but friendly manner. Jack had a flash of muscular bare legs as she scooted back to make room for him. He looked away politely, but smelled her musk and something sweet and light on her breath anyway, and in the dim light she could have been almost anyone at all.

"Name's Polly. Glad to be of service." She lifted something toward his face, and Jack groaned with unexpected pleasure. It was a small, battery-operated fan that blew hard enough to dry the sweat on his brow, if only for the moment that she held it there. "After that horror show across the road, I don't want to be alone." Polly turned the fan to her own skin, then back to Jack. "I hope you don't mind."

"I'm not bothered either way." He drew his knees up and folded his arms around them. His stomach pressed against his thighs. His armpits were soaked through.

"Aren't you hot in that shirt?" Polly asked. "You'd have to be, wouldn't you."

Instead of answering her question, which in her indefinable accent was clearly not, Jack sniffed. "Did you yell earlier? It was you, wasn't it?" He was fairly sure it had been her, and wasn't surprised when she looked sheepish.

"Sorry about that. I was having bad dreams." She laughed at herself. "We all get those here."

"Not me."

"Right on. What's it like in the presidential suite?"

Jack remained silent, the answer obvious. Polly went on as though it weren't.

"I could've had your room. But I took one look—no screens, no nets, ensuite bath with cracks around all the water pipes coming in, and that bloody awful boiler steaming away above the tub—and I told Mr. N'gon to get stuffed." Her voice was loud in the small space, a reassurance to herself, or so Jack thought. "You'll know better next time." She pulled out a bag of fruit and began to peel a brown, lumpish thing that in the dark resembled a tumor. "Want some?"

"What else've you got?"

"Um, let's see. Sacs of jackfruit, a dragonfruit, a bunch of longans. And this custard apple. Here, open up—"

She ripped off a piece and thrust it toward Jack's face, her fingers dripping with juice. It smelled sweet and he opened his mouth and took it from her. It tasted like crystallized honey, and between them, the fruit disappeared very quickly. Polly opened another, and they ate that as well. After it was gone, they sat in contemplative silence until the clamorous impact of something very big collapsing at the end of the alley shook the floor of their room and startled them both into drawing closer together.

Jack almost put his arm around Polly's shoulder—a father's old instinct—but he caught himself. "This place is coming apart at the seams."

"Growing pains."

"Sure. Can I ask you something?"

"Sure."

"Where will you be next week?"

"Next week?"

"Yeah. Or next month or next year?"

Polly tilted her head, as though the answer should be obvious. "Right here. This place is very healthy for me." She began to peel a spiny, ruffled, neon-pink oblong that could only be the dragonfruit. It tasted like a kiwi that had expended all of its energy on its gaudy clothes and had little left to flavor its flesh, but to Jack, it also tasted like coolness somehow.

"Healthy? It is?"

"Sure." Polly brushed a shock of damp hair from her forehead. "Before I came here, I was quite the little twinkie—soft and pale and mass-produced. Looking like I spent my life watching other people live theirs. But you couldn't guess that by looking at me now."

Jack agreed. The silhouettes of her forearms were netted with veins; her face was chiseled by deft cuts out of the humid darkness. "But is it safe?"

She laughed. "Are you kidding? This is Cambodia!"

Jack didn't know how to take her comment, but opted not to ask for fear of confirming what he already believed to be true. He thought about returning to his room. His face must have betrayed him, because Polly put her sticky hand on his.

"Tell you what. You can crash here, if you want. It'll be cool with the window open. I don't mind. And next time, you'll know better."

"Nightmares, huh?" Jack nodded but she looked concerned that he might leave anyway, so he stretched out beside her, their bodies apart but their heads almost touching. The bed was small and damp with the girl's sweat, but after his stifling, empty room, it was fine. "I don't know what you mean."

They lay in silence for a while. Jack stopped sweating, but his forehead, cooled whenever the breeze touched it, soon turned hot again. He thought Polly had gone to sleep—her breathing was very regular and slow—and was almost at that point himself, when she spoke as quickly and enthusiastically as though she had been doing nothing more slumberous than saving up her strength.

"They stole their blood, did you know that? Tied them down like the Christ and bled them until they were almost gone. Then they chucked them in their pits, buried them alive at Cheung Ek and gave their blood to injured Khmer Rouge."

"Could we talk about something else?"

"Like what?"

"Like what you're doing here, Polly? If you've discarded your home and your past, what will you write on your clean slate?"

Polly gasped, the possibilities uncountable in such a wild country. "I might teach English at a rural school. Hell, I might *build* a rural school! Some guys from San Francisco are working upcountry rehabilitating a village. Putting in a well, teaching them how to raise pigs, that sort of thing. Might go and dig that for a while."

"You'd feel safe doing that? A girl like you?"

Polly rolled onto her side and peered at Jack in the darkness from a distance of several inches. "Why are you so concerned with my safety?"

"I'm not."

She thought about this for a moment. "Where did you come from?"

"Vermont. I always bitch about it, God help me, the cold, the tourists, but I miss it a great deal right now. Skiing. Cold, your breath in plumes. Air like shards of glass, sour and metallic and *vast* in your nose. Watching the leaves turn from my front porch with my wife." He draped the back of a hand over his eyes as though suffering from a migraine. "With my daughter, on the really good days."

Polly made a happy noise, and fell silent. Her breathing slowed. Jack began to doze.

"Cut off fingers, flayed them. Did you see their signs?" Polly cried out. She squinted and grabbed an imaginary neck before her, throttling the air. "*You are a chap who has dared to thwart the revolution.* Unbelievable!"

"Shut up!" Jack said. "No wonder you have nightmares. God." He rubbed his eyes.

"You sure don't like it here, do you?" Polly asked.

"My daughter apparently does." The words slipped out before he could bite them back, and Polly clapped—small, sharp punctures of the silence that pressed against the shroud.

"Right on! What's she doing? Who's she with?"

Jack sighed. He hadn't meant to say anything at all, not to this girl who was close enough to his daughter's age to acutely remind him of her frailty and vulnerability. "No one. She came with friends from college, but they called me last month and told me she'd lost her mind and wasn't coming home. Then she shot off a few emails, cashed the money I wired her for new tickets—she'd sold her onward tickets if you can believe that—and a decent hotel. That's the last I heard from Claire."

"What did she say?"

"That she had notified her school of her intention to drop out. That she had important work to do." Jack cleared his throat. "That she thought she had fallen in love. Polly, when I was your age, we were all trying to make something of ourselves, instead of throwing everything away as fast as we could."

"We have enough."

"You're living on your parents' money."

Polly didn't seem offended, just curious. "How do you know what I'm living on?"

"Because that's what missionaries do. And artists and poets and writers and the others that chase vaguely romantic vocations that nobody pays them to do."

"Whose fault is that? Whose fault is any of it? You make our world into a place where a lot of us don't want to participate."

Jack didn't want to argue with her. His gut tightened, presumably from the fruit, which, now that he thought about it, might have been a little too sweet. Spoiled. "I was sure I'd find her in Siem Reap. That's her speed, you see. Drinking, partying, tourist temples like Angkar Wat."

"*Angkor.*"

"Who cares how it's pronounced?"

"Big difference between Angkor and Angkar. Your daughter would care." She laughed. "Because you raised her right."

"Oh, just shut the hell up. Are your lives so empty back home that you'd throw them away so quickly?"

"It doesn't matter why we do it, Jack, as long as someone's doing it." She rolled over. "Because it sure as hell isn't you."

"I have a family."

"So do they."

"You all are nothing but relief junkies, getting high on other peoples' suffering. It's a parent's nightmare."

"Your life is our nightmare, your

scrabbling, your greed. That's why your daughter will be here for a while."

"And how would you know that?

"It gets into your head, being here."

"No, it doesn't. Not if you don't let it." Jack sat up, unwilling to stay any longer with this girl, but unable to force himself to return to his steamy room. "I'll wait her out in Siem Reap. Come tomorrow morning, I'm gone as fast as I can get a taxi to Pochentong Airport."

"There aren't any taxis that stay in this part of town, you know. Only motos, cyclos, and tuk-tuks."

"Oh for the love of Christ."

Polly let out a long breath with a soft hum in her throat. "So I met this girl down on the beach a few hours from here. She's Australian, been there for years. She runs a charity, almost got me to stay down there with her. This other one, Samantha, is up the river in Kratie. She wants to save the dolphins! Been in-country since she was seventeen." Her fingertips settled delicately on her breast. "For me, it's only been a few months, but I hope to change that slowly. In fact, just in talking with you I've decided to stay at least three years, eight months and twenty days."

"Good god! Your parents will kill

themselves! What's the matter with you?"

Polly shook her head slowly, her eyes dazed as though she briefly pondered Jack's question, and had found something was the matter after all. "It's an amount of time that every Khmer knows by heart. I want to know it too."

"If you hadn't noticed, I'm not a Khmer. I'm a dentist."

Her voice was cracked and flat, a young girl suddenly exhausted. "That's how long *they* were here. The KR. The oppressors." Polly lifted her hand from where it rested on the sliver of her stomach. In the dark it looked like a crazed bird as she threw her fingers in the direction of Toul Sleng.

"Don't wait for your daughter, Jack. She isn't coming home."

You must sign the confession, Brother. Without it, you will not be allowed to die.

What will they do?

Not so loud! You don't want to know what I heard.

Please, Brother, I must know.

There are three groups. Mild, hot, and rabid. In this barrack we are all to meet A'Nân. He is in charge of the Rabid Group. I'm sorry, Brother.

What will happen then?

39

It depends on the interrogator. Some whip, others use electricity. Some hold you underwater. A'Nân, he will cut your fingers off or peel the skin from your back. You must tell him everything.

I don't know anything!

You will have to convince him otherwise.

But there are children here! A girl in the next row! What can Angkar learn from a six-year-old girl?

You don't want to know what they will learn from her, Brother. Before they destroy her, Angkar will know her inside and out.

Jack awakened to a sound like someone gasping, a strangled little sound that filled the pit of his stomach with terror. In the heartbeat of pure silence that followed, there was an aural blackness deeper than anything his eyes had experienced even here, in this place. The noise came again, louder and wetter. This time it was accompanied by a sudden pain in his leg, and Jack scooted backward in a momentary panic before realizing what the matter was. With more care than he had expected, he worked Polly's fingers loose from the skin and hairs on his thigh where she had clenched them in her unknown panic, and slipped quietly from beneath the netting.

Everyone has nightmares here. It wasn't yet

ten at night. He felt nauseous. Why did he come to this country at all, instead of staying home and waiting for his daughter to come to her senses? Should he fly back to Siem Reap to see if she'd turned up yet, or would it be just another waste of time? The guesthouse was enveloped by a pure black silence, and in it, Jack's soft curse emerged as the brittle whine of a child. How could she want to stay in a place like this? Why didn't she realize that she was throwing her life away, like the girl beneath the shroud?

Behind him, in her dark room, Polly gasped again as though she were suffocating, and he couldn't help but imagine if his daughter's nights were spent like this.

Your life is our nightmare. As he padded back to his room, Jack could feel the floor sink and warp beneath his tender, bare feet, giving him the impression that he was held by these thinnest wood slats not above a sleepy eatery, but above a yawning black drop.

What is your age?
　　　Twenty two, Brother A'Nân.
　　　Where did you grow up?
　　　Siem Reab, Brother A'Nân.
　　　What were the names of your friends?
　　　I didn't have any, Brother.

What did you do during the reign of Sihanouk?

I was a student, nothing more, Brother.

During Lon Nol, then?

I was a laborer. I have done nothing, Brother. You must believe me.

Do you think Angkar is stupid? Angkar does not make mistakes, and it does not catch people who are not guilty! Now think of what you may have done wrong.

I cannot.

With whom did you collaborate to betray Angkar?

No one, Brother.

When did you first instigate people who would destroy Angkar?

I did no such thing, Brother.

Confess the number of people in your network!

I have no network!

So you worked alone to aid the kmang *to undermine Angkar?*

No, Brother!

Perhaps if I bleed your head you will recall your crimes.

The screaming was an unearthly sound like a cat dying or a child being strangled by his father. Jack jerked upright in the darkness, his chest aching, his scalp drenched with blood.

"This can't be good, oh Christ this can't be good," he muttered, wiping his brow with his bare arm. It came away dripping. He twisted the flashlight on above the bed. The pool of light swung back and forth around him, its color ripening; his shadow danced and jittered, softer around its edges now, it too, trying to escape. Soon it would vanish entirely. He ran his fingers through his hair, and then checked them by the light. They glistened, but they hadn't come away red, as he had expected.

The animal noise that had awakened him from his fitful, heatstroke sleep faded to an echo in his ears, and Jack picked himself up from the sodden sheets. Like the Khmers on the streets, this house was old enough to have heard screams like that once. Who had lived in here? It had likely been deserted. From some hidden place in his head that collected information without his bidding, he recalled that the Khmer Rouge had evacuated everyone into the countryside. It was more likely that the house had belonged to the upper cadre, the ones who did the deeds. In either case, he was beginning to believe in the memory of place, the shadows of the past burned against the walls.

He could feel the gray hulk of Toul Sleng beside his room. It was just across the narrow alley, where the same thin brown men still waited for their victims. When he put his hand on the cinder wall, he could feel the clump of feet and the drag of chains. He could hear the trucks coming day and night, emptying, filling, rumbling over potholed tracks bound for the killing fields. He could hear the sounds of iron bars slapping motionless flesh, and hear the wailing mothers as their children were sawn in half.

Jack paced alongside the bed, but it was no use. He didn't have to fall asleep to hear them anymore.

Although you implicated no others, your confession is accepted, Brother. After the doctors bandage your wounds, you will be provided with transportation to your new home. Do not worry, Brother. Your wife and daughter are there already.

Now, you will stay in this hut until someone comes to collect you. Give him your name when he asks, and do not remove your blindfold. Do not be alarmed at the sound of the generator. It is loud, but necessary.

Come, Brother. Stand here. Someone will remove your blindfold in a moment. Never mind the smell. It is only dead cows beside the road. Kneel down, Brother. Keep your hands behind your back. Do not move, and do not forget—Angkar is proud of your loyalty. This is only a precaution for our safety.

The power came on with a lurch—a vibration that came up through the floor and returned life to the appliances. Lights came on, both in the main room and the bathroom. The colors of the kitchen beneath the window, gold and blue, bleached out to the faded white of bones. The air conditioner's slats resumed their languid oscillations above the bed, and icy air erupted from its throat as though that small black slit led to the high country of Vermont.

Jack left the lights on as he gasped like a fish in the cold stream, letting it flow over his drenched back and down his sides. He lay like that for a very long time, and then, without him being aware that it was so, morning came and he awoke.

Snails of the South Pacific

The young boy rested on his back amid the long swell, surrounded by the blue of an ocean at the boundary of its shallows and the place of storms. There was a smear of white and green in the distance—his home, an island somewhere chronologically behind Pitcairn, beneath the Marquises and above Marotiri; Mathow couldn't have said where, exactly. It was at the confluence of two great currents of water twisting their way from one horizon to the other, and that was enough for him.

He floated with the ease of a sea otter under the obese equatorial sun and Gauguin's dabs of purple and red. The slanted light made the water dark shades of pelagic blue, and wavelets marched along the surface, small and confused by a weak, distant depression. They slapped rhythmically against the sides of his face and shoaled across his hairless brown chest. There were seventy feet of water at his back, the depth rendering a color very like the bellies of the clouds gathering on the horizon. It stole into to his ears, filling them up and muting the sounds of the surface—moaning wind and pattering wavelets and the sound of the bell in the middle of Ai Oaiha harbor, distant and faraway. But beneath his small body and the sound of his heart he could hear other noises rising from those gelid depths: distant groans that reminded him of crusty old whales and flaccid, sharp-smelling squid, all painted over the ancient undertone of endlessly shifting sand and the swaying of the kelp. It was the home of stonefish and sharks, sea snakes and strange fish with beaks the size of his fist who spun mucous cocoons around their bodies each night while they slept.

This was the right place; he was sure of it. After years of begging and spying, it was only this morning that his older brother had revealed to him the location of the hidden sandfield that lay below him now. *The corals are so sharp they cut your hand to the bone, sharks so plentiful the sky is blocked out when you down there. The currents kill you quick, suck you over the shelf and into the deep. But, oh, the hunting! The snails get so big you never seen nothing like it. They older than you, little brother. Older than me, some of them.*

All around, the night was fast approaching

Mathow's little island. By the time he had found the beach with the markers his brother had let slip—for his brother had forbidden Mathow to come to this place until he was older—the sun was low and deeply red. Not having a dinghy of his own, Mathow had been forced to make the swim past the lip of the shallow coral atoll, and locate the proper spot by trial and error—*Mahai's hut lines up with the headland between the split palms on the beach, little brother, and then straight down to the bottom of the sea*—and so he had been able to make only three descents before his lungs felt like leather bags. Worst of all, he had caught nothing, not even a glimpse of his prey. Now, he had only the light left for one last dive.

He rolled over in the water. The light was too angled for him to see much below. His stomach grumbled—he had skipped lunch in his excitement to get started—but he felt just strong enough for one last try.

After a moment spent calming himself, his hands snapped together beneath him, pushing his head high above the water. He drew three shallow breaths followed by one single, sharp inhalation, and then his legs were above the surface, kicking air and cooled suddenly by the breeze. Mathow shivered, and before becoming aware that he had done so, the weight of his legs above the surface arrowed him down. After holding his arms fast before his body for several seconds, he began to pull against the water rhythmically, hands first outstretched and then flat against his sides and then reaching into the deepening blue again.

Mathow slid from his surface thoughts like a snake slides from its summer skin—his gnawing hunger, his scalded lungs, the pretty cousin he wanted to kiss, all gone. These thoughts were replaced by deepening colors, the sound of the pulse in his ears, the warmth in his chest. His eighteen-year-old facemask was too large for his sharp face, and as he moved deeper, rivulets of seawater began to seep along the lines of his temples. He ignored the salty trickle, exhaling through his nostrils into the mask every so often to counter the growing pressure of the sea against both the glass and his eardrums. He moved smoothly and gracefully, his legs scissoring, thick curls of black hair streaming from the oval of his face. In the waistband of his bright green shorts he carried the twelve-inch flathead screwdriver he had borrowed from his Uncle's workshop; his feet trailed small silvery bubbles.

The seabed surrounding the volcanic atoll fell steeply away into the depths, the igneous rock crusty and sharp, as the bottom tended to be around such South Pacific islands. There were trenches not far from here so deep that a steel object thrown from a canoe would sink for days before it touched bottom, and when it did, it would be nothing but a crushed hulk. Mathow's boyish imagination had no difficulties imagining how the inky currents his brother had warned him of might easily suck him into such deadly depths, or worse still, drown him within sight of the rippling mercury boundary of the air.

Deeper still, the water grew chilled with a wretched suddenness. Light and color were eaten by the depth, which stole the heat of the sunset and turned it into the terribly vacant yet expectant blue of the open ocean. Shapes loomed from this blue, elongated silvery fishes, but as yet no sharks. The boy continued his methodical pulling of the water.

After an interminable time, a blip of whiteness came into focus, swimming from the edge of his vision until it filled it. As his toes sank into the cold sand, as he had done the previous three dives, he paused.

On one side of him, the volcanic rock and corals that formed the island soared away toward the invisible surface. On the other, the world fell into black abysmal depths. At the boundary of the black water, Mathow could see specks of material, fishes and krill, swept along the edge of the sandfield in a shallow arc, in sight only for an instant before disappearing like a conveyor into the deep. Between these suddenly terrifying extremes lay the sandfield, and the abalone he had come to hunt.

Underwater for forty-five seconds already, the boy had expended a great deal of energy and oxygen. He knew that he had perhaps thirty seconds before he had to kick off for the surface. Mathow began to move forward.

The sandfield was strewn with boulders, some no larger than betel nuts scattered between others that thrust upward from the bottom like teeth to tower blackly higher than the hut in which Mathow slept. As he swam slowly amid their stately gloom, the boy found it difficult to focus, for swimming this water was like sinking upward, untethered, into a moonlit sky. He began to pretend that he was only in the blue shallows of the lagoon after sundown and after a while, he forgot his depth and his heartbeat calmed enough so that he was able to scan the rocks methodically, as his brother had taught him.

The rocks were rich with all manner of life—anemone that would have been a brilliant crimson at the surface but at this depth were a coaly gray, a pulsing eel gasping at the entrance to his den, schools of nervous little fish. Eyes watched from cracks in the stone and from bodies buried beneath the sand. But, as on the previous three dives, he could see no abalone.

It wasn't surprising—they were mossy and wonderfully camouflaged—but even so he had expected to see at least a few in such a mythical spot. He continued on, moving purposefully over the bigger rocks, combing them with a deliberate gaze, clearing his mask once, and then again. He saw nothing.

Then, just as Mathow was ready to kick for the surface in disgust, he saw it. His eyes creased into a hunter's squint.

Shaped by strong tidal currents and living coral, the rock stood monolithic, a giant axe-head broken off in the white sand, almost entirely covered by the swirling green blades of sea lettuce. Medusas waved along small ledges, and scallops watched with indigo-rimmed eyes.

The circular shell was almost entirely hidden by waving sea creatures as it moved slowly halfway down the stony surface, looking like nothing so much as a peasant's hat, complete with waving jelly hairs poking from beneath. Judging by its size, the abalone had been filtering algae from the phosphorescent waters for perhaps twenty years or more; the largest of them, his brother had told him once, were half a century old. Ten inches across, the abalone moved slowly on its muscular foot, unaware of the approaching danger.

Mathow wasted no time. He drew his arm back to jam the blade of the screwdriver beneath the perimeter of the shell. His hand flashed forward, and the blade struck something impenetrable and then stuck there.

Mathow scissored his legs twice, hard, to keep his position, and shook his head.

His mistake had been simple and avoidable. In his zeal, he had thrust forward too quickly, hoping to disable the giant mollusk with an immediately fatal blow. Instead, he had missed the narrow gap between the shell and the rock, and the abalone, sensing the sudden swirl of water over its filters, retracted his foot and hugged the rock with the always desperate force of prey. Had he slipped the screwdriver in slowly and accurately, the snail would be in his hand. Now, however, the abalone had become a part of the rock.

Tantalizingly close, the mollusk hunkered amid the waving sea lettuce. Undaunted, Mathow held the screwdriver in both hands and began to work it back and forth. He began slowly, careful not to lose his grip, sliding the blade deeper a millimeter at a time. Blood pounded in Mathow's temples from the effort; his arms shook and his fingers began to cramp. He cursed the fact that he was small, and that he had no knife, whose blade he could twist and so apply more pressure. But he never once cursed his quarry.

Finally, there came an almost imperceptible lifting of the shell, a vacuum broken somewhere, and then, the snail tore free of the rock. The abalone fluttered toward the pale sand like a falling leaf, coming to rest on its shell, the white muscle of its foot scalloped and loose at the edges.

The effects of the sudden release of tension on Mathow were immediate—he tumbled away from the rock and toward the edge of the sandfield like a man tumbling into the depths of space. As the shelf fell away beneath him, he felt the dreaded wall current, icy from its eleven thousand foot rise from the ocean bottom, first tousle, and then seize, his legs. It flipped him upside down in an instant, and dragged him down. His old mask loosened and flooded, and the abalone was forgotten.

The water grew immediately black in the lee of the wall, which stretched into an infinitely thicker darkness. Mathow was a Polynesian swimmer, but even he was helpless against the sucking currents; at almost eight knots, they were simply too strong. He was ground against outcroppings of coral as he was swept down the plunging wall like a piece of kelp.

Without hesitating, Mathow speared his right hand into a cleft in the coral and balled his fingers into a fist. The skin tore almost immediately, and he briefly worried about the schooling whitetip reef sharks and hammerheads that he knew hunted here. His right elbow and shoulder twisted painfully, and his legs flapped loosely behind him, but his strength held. It had to. If it didn't, he would never see the surface again.

After a moment to digest the pain, Mathow began to pull himself fist over fist up the coral until the wall crested and he felt himself slip from the grip of the currents. He managed the last few feet and almost sighed in relief, until he realized that there were twelve fathoms still bearing down upon him.

Mathow was drowning. Of course he had been drowning slowly for the whole of this undersea hunt, but the excitement, the exertion and the depth finally made themselves known in the fire in his chest. But he knew if he surfaced, his first kill (which was still very much alive) would vanish into the dark cracks or beneath the sand.

The decision was made in an instant, and Mathow returned to where he had last seen the snail, helpless, overturned like a turtle on its shell. It wasn't there anymore.

Mathow stared stupidly at the place below the rim of the rock where the snail had fallen, convinced that his eyes were mistaken. He moved into the deep shadow of the rock, sifting the sand through his fingers as though perhaps the mollusk had dug its way into the earth, but there was no trace of it.

He quickly cleared his mask and peered into the deep shadows beneath the overhanging rock, and realized what must have happened. In the amount of time it had taken Mathow to battle the deadly current and claw his way back to the sandfield, the abalone had righted itself and was even now crawling unerringly beneath the base of the axe, where it would wedge its horny shell against the stone above. Then, there would be no force that could dislodge it.

Frantically, Mathow lunged forward beneath the rock. It scraped against his back, and the sand pressed upward on his chest, but almost against his conscious will, his legs kicked him ever forward into tighter spaces, his arms scrabbling, pushing with his elbows and digging into the sand. Now, with outstretched fingers, he could just brush the old snail as it hurried (at the pace of an old snail) ever closer to safety.

There was no light so deep under the rock. Mathow blindly swept his hand across the sand, undeterred by the sheer variety of marine creatures which might live beneath the rock and which could do him serious injury. Stonefish, eels, cone shells, anemones, fire corals, dinural and very deadly seasnakes that were just now waking up—the list was too long to worry about now. There was almost no room to move now, but Mathow, with a young hunter's bravery and stupidity, wriggled forward another foot. Nothing. Another forward thrust of his legs, into the deadly vise of coral and sand.

It was enough.

The abalone lurched drunkenly beneath his hand as Mathow pressed it into the sand, slowing its motion, but the abalone was experienced—he wasn't fooled into trying futilely to scrabble for purchase on the soft surface. It wanted stone. Now and again, Mathow felt the tickle of the abalone's eyes, those waving stalks of jelly, brush against his skin, but finally he centered his palm over the thickness of the shell, and began to pull the abalone back. It came toward him a few inches, and Mathow knew he had won.

He tried to push back from beneath the rock, and realized that he was stuck.

He refused to release the old snail; he had worked far too hard to justify doing so in his mind. Instead, he gripped it tighter, wincing as he felt his skin part at the place where the edge of the shell came across it. At the sight of his own blood in the water—strangely greenish at this depth—all fear fled him then, and with his free hand, he pushed at the rock that held him, wedged him against the sand. He pushed with all of his fading strength, and felt his green shorts ripping along the backside. Gouges that would take weeks to heal appeared along the backs of his legs and shoulders. His head throbbed, and his vision dimmed.

Then, with a surge of water, he was in the open. As he righted himself, and prepared to shove off the bottom, he saw them.

At first, he thought the dark, mossy blobs peppering the boulders were spots of blood in his eyes or artifacts from oxygen deprivation. He shook his head, unable to believe what he was seeing—abalone, hundreds of them, gliding over the rocks with a snail's inexorable pace. Eyestalks waved from under coral outcrops and from beneath the sand.

Mathow shook his head. They must have been there the whole time, he thought slowly, but then he ran out of time. Underwater for almost two minutes now, he pushed off. Mathow's feet sank into the sand as he kicked away from the bottom with all the strength left in his legs. His mask tore away his eyes, raked over his nose, and flopped madly back and forth around his neck. He ignored it, and kept his eyes open.

The conflagration grew within his hitching chest. Denied air, each gasp felt as though his lungs were collapsing into themselves, shriveled bloody sacks, but diving in the lagoon had taught him a few tricks, ways to fool the body. There were still thirty feet of water above his head when the boy began to empty his lungs, and he lost the surface in a net of glistening silver. Immediately he felt a little better as he flew upward toward the light.

As the tremendous pressure began to ease, as the air remaining in his burning lungs continued to expand, he could feel the abalone's sticky foot pulsing in his fist, followed by a nasty sensation as the old snail desperately chafed at the boy's skin with his rasp tongue, back and forth, back and forth. Mathow clasped the pumice of the shell with bleeding fingers, tightly and now with both hands. Caught in a rising mass of his own spent air, he was hurtling upward, legs churning, eyes stinging from the water that pushed into the corners of his eyes.

Faster and faster he rose. The water became ever lighter, and colors swam back one by one, the rainbow returning in reverse. Twenty feet from the surface his lungs were empty; fifteen feet, and his vision grew dim. Ten feet now, shoulders tensed, hands once again separated, one stroking in long draws of water as the other used the abalone as a paddle, hands up over his head now and five feet coming fast and he pulled his arms down in one final violent stroke and then he broke the shimmering surface and kept rising into the evening sky, propelled out of the water rising like a dolphin, floating into the last of the sunshine and into air that tasted like palms and tide pools, leaving the terrible coldness behind and deep below, a tableau teeming with fish and sharks and strange snails watching with a million eyes in the dark.

Mathow swam blindly to shore with burning eyes and rubber arms, cutting through the wavelets with a jerky jellyfish sidestroke. He pulled himself out of the water and collapsed on the sand, glowing red just above the waterline.

Without thought, he hooked his fingers into his prize. The shell ripped away with a sound like a foot slipping from mud, and the old snail gave one final spastic contraction as it died. Relaxed, it overflowed the boy's brown hand with its benthic pallor. It smelled like the sea as the abalone hunter brought the white flesh to his lips, and ate.

TRAVELING ON TRAINS

Nick Gregory hunched cross-legged on his narrow berth, rummaging through the contents of his new blue backpack. Inside were three shirts, an extra pair of pants, undergarments, toiletries, a novel, a picture of a woman, but he pushed these aside to get to the dog-eared guidebook tucked within the folds of fabric at the bottom. He refilled the pack and moved it to the head of his bunk where it would serve as his pillow, but for now, although it was almost midnight in this Beijing August night, hot enough to reach through the black window and press the shirt wetly against his shoulders and down his back, he didn't lie down to rest.

All the lights on the old Chinese train were dim; the one in his compartment especially so. It guttered like candlelight and caused shadows to jitter madly in the corners and along the walls. Nick turned the guide over—Jane's old Lonely Planet—and rested it on his thigh, wondering why his wife had come this way. The coal-mining outpost of Datong was serviced only by this poor, rattling sleeper that took its luckless passengers to China's heavily-industrialized hinterland, yet there was a flurry of entries around it in Jane's guidebook, written in the margins in her careful, round script. Nick flipped through forests of exclamation points that had sprouted beside circled attractions, and peered, suddenly bleary, at shaky shapes that could have been hearts that embraced hotels on the outskirts of town. Red-ink arrows led to a monastery that clung to a cliff like an egg case; caves around here were filled with asterisks and carvings of the Buddha. Like Jane's crumb-trail in Beijing, these would be Nick's next destinations as well.

In this compartment that smelled of smoke and old shirts, Nick thought the same thoughts he did each time his large, ungainly feet trod upon the memories of Jane's smaller steps. What had she been thinking as this Chinese train had pulled out of Beijing almost a year ago to the day? On what details had her gaze lingered? There were few choices, all of which he'd considered but would now consider again. Four bunks, two to a side and three of them empty. A metal table beneath a black window caked with coal dust. A white doily on the table, a flattened aluminum bowl. Clipped to the table's base, a battered steel thermos filled with boiled water. Faded blue tapestries. The dim yellow light.

Nick knew better, though, on what his wife's gaze had lingered. He cleared his throat and closed his eyes, as though feigning a headache or having something to say.

When he'd first found his place on the train, thoughts of his wife had overcome him, and he'd carefully touched the overhead panels, spun the blades of the stalled fan. He'd peered beneath the lower bunks, and put his nose against the windowpane at the height he figured the nose of a woman about five five might have reached.

The train gave a lurch, and Nick checked his watch. Eight hours to memorize these details before fresh ones came to steal them away.

The train sagged beneath compartment upon compartment filled with passengers snoring and farting, twitching bare feet cantilevered from the edges of bunks. Small men in undershirts hunched over bowls of food, slurping without glancing up. Babies slept in laps.

But to Nick's surprise, his compartment remained empty as the train pulled out of the station amidst much metallic groaning and screeching, rolling through lazy bends in the tracks and then picking up a little speed. The motion was like a hammock or a ship in good weather, and he lay back, head propped against his pack, shoes off and feet crossed at the ankles. After pressing the spine of the guide against his jaw as though pressure were needed there to relieve the ache of a tooth, he briefly exchanged it for the novel. It was a recent habit; back home he had never been much of a reader of fiction, but this book had belonged to Jane, so he would read it through. Right now, though, the words were running together as they sometimes did, and he lay the book face down on his chest. He closed his eyes. Jane was waiting for him there.

She was returning from a voyage, a bag in her hand, and a look on her face that made him awaken.

Wait, it wasn't that at all.

His eyes flew open and a wave of disorientation surged over him in the darkness. The train was stalled. Voices were raised outside, and the sound of feet slapping along the corridors and fists banging on doors that were still distant, but coming closer, caused Nick to claw blindly behind his head. The yellow light that before had seemed so ineffectual now beat back the shadows and filled him with relief. It was short-lived.

After a second of silence during which Nick could count his pulse in his ears, someone hammered on the slider. Without pause, the hasp began to joggle back and forth, and then it shot back on its own. No sooner had it done so, the slider sprung open with a shriek and a woman in railway uniform and bearing a stony look on her face thrust her head into the compartment. Before he could open his mouth at the intrusion, Nick saw the shadows on the wall behind her, and realized that she wasn't alone. When the shadows came to life, Nick winced.

Two people brushed past the attendant and swept into the compartment with the assurance of those unaccustomed to being slowed. One of them was a short, stout man about thirty years of age. He wore a plain white T-shirt that struggled to cover his round belly, and brown shorts that revealed a scar flowing down one chubby leg from inside the thigh past the kneecap like a dried red and black zipper. The edges of the wound were still angry, and small scabs dotted where hundreds of stitches had recently been removed. In one thickset hand he carried a large black duffle; the other arm was draped around a woman younger than he, and dressed in a purple shirt tucked deeply into high, baggy slacks. She was thin, with a symmetrical face and a strong jaw, and as she helped the man limp inside, Nick decided that she bore a resemblance to Jane. He wasn't surprised; these days, most women did.

The man's scar was as terrible as the woman's face was arresting, but neither of these things gave Nick a shudder. That was done easily, and accompanied by no small measure of dismay, by the black-billed, octagonal green cap that each of them wore on their heads. He'd seen enough of them milling among the crowded platzes and squares of Beijing. Worn by people at whom nobody dared stare for too long, those caps left no doubt as to the identity of the wearers—soldiers of the Red Chinese Army.

The train jerked to life and pulled back into the night.

Over the years Nick had seen footage from China, from Tien An Men. He'd heard the dissidents' tales at the hands of people like the ones who now were bustling inches below him. As he took air silently through an open mouth, his mind churned with things to do, things that maybe he shouldn't do—eye contact, rustling the pages of his book too loudly, drawing their attention—but his curiosity got the better of him and he hazarded a look over the edge.

Instantly, as though sensing a shadow crossing the face of the sun, they froze, straightened, and turned sharply. Not knowing what else to do, Nick cleared his throat and greeted them with some of the only Mandarin he remembered.

"*Nee ho mah.*"

The soldiers regarded each other for a painful moment before the man turned back to Nick. "*Eh, hen hao! Ni ne.*"

Nick thought he would burst into laughter. For weeks before Jane's trip, she had driven him half-crazy pacing through rooms reciting hypothetical dialogues in Mandarin: *Hi! How are you? Well. Hi! How are you? Well, thanks. Hi! How are you? Very well, thanks. Hi! How are you? Fucking super, and you?* That last, she shouted in English, laughing, her knees together but her feet apart. Now, as the soldier cocked his head and awaited his answer, from that memory of his wife Nick gathered that the man had said *Very well, and you?*

Nick nodded. "*Hao, xie xie.*"

The first contact must have been a success because the soldier broke into a wide, double-chinned grin. It was a goofy look for the man, but no doubt a familiar one, for his face fell into deep creases beneath the eyes and around his mouth. The woman rolled her eyes, and the corners of her lips tightened into the ghost of a wry upward curl.

As the soldiers unpacked, Nick pretended

to busy himself in the guidebook, but in reality he continued to watch them over the tops of the pages.

After pulling a magazine from her small bag, the woman stretched out on the lower bunk and began to thumb through its pages. The man had other plans. He unzipped his tote, and Nick's stomach gave a startled squeeze at the suddenly heavy smell of food. He lifted the guidebook and tried to tune out the sounds from below with thoughts from before.

His stomach clenched again and Nick kneaded at it even as his mouth pulled itself into a rueful grin. Like many other parts of him—his ability to act in company, his ability to laugh or to even see a future for himself—the small potbelly Jane had once found endearing had left.

Three weeks spent tracing Jane's movements through sooty alleyways and across vast concrete palaces of Beijing hadn't cleared his head or given him any insight as he had hoped it might. In fact, it had only made things worse. He began to get the sense that she was always within each pagoda, until it became unbearable and he would dart inside to find nothing but shadows and dusty furniture. He began to see her dark hair flying, on women standing with their backs to him or on bicycles always flying fast.

Meanwhile, other frustrations mounted. His ignorance of the language rendered him virtually mute. It also prevented him from feeding himself properly. He couldn't seem to find dishes he could keep down—a bowl of soup ordered from the commissary tonight had brimmed with greasy fish skins and hunks of eel, but he'd tried anyway; he didn't want to go scavenging for finger-bananas and mealy apples like he had the night before. But the fire in the syrupy liquid had coated his tongue and throat and put a quick end to the attempt. Looking now at his ribs, his wrists and the knobs of his knees, he guessed he was down twenty pounds. Nothing to do about that, Nick thought, except head on toward a little town built of carbon and monuments, where, upon her return last spring, Jane had told him of the importance of finding something hidden and good in the face of adversity. He wondered if that last had been solely for his benefit, for then only she had known the nature of adversity that would soon be facing her husband.

The soldier barked a hearty laugh, and Nick rolled to the edge of the bunk.

The duffle lay deflated between the soldier's feet, its contents arrayed on the table and the floor around it. Nick's mouth grew wet at the sight of so much food. The variety present was as amazing as it was endless. Nick could identify several of the items—flaky pastries and chips, prunes, hard-boiled eggs—but as surely as the soups hiding razor bones and coagulated clots of blood, he knew these were liars, too. The prunes would be salted; the chips were made from squid. The pastries, so serene and golden brown, were filled with pigeons, and the eggs hid their charges of boiled ducklings well until the first bite. Nick ignored these. The rest, however, were more mysterious, and so held greater promise. They came wrapped in paper and in tubes and cans, in jars and in a little figurine with a screw-off head. The final item to be grandly whipped from the duffel: a huge plastic bag containing a tangle of something gnarled and knobby like winter branches.

The man pulled open the two halves of the bag, and the thick smell of smoked chicken feet immediately caught Nick's nose even through the layer of carbon that had built up in his sinuses during his stay in Beijing. The man took a foot and began to eat it. Nick sniffed deeply, and the soldier lifted the bag over his head.

Nick stared at it dumbly until it dawned on him that the soldier had been observing him the entire time, and was now offering to share. All the while he held the bag out, the soldier continued to chew, and the sound of hollow bones crunching between his teeth withered the idea. "Um, *bu yao*," Nick managed. The soldier shrugged his round shoulders and grabbed another foot. He poked it, toes first, into his mouth and bit down. The sound of the cracking bones was similar in its effect on Nick to fingernails on a blackboard, but the man's face registered a deep satisfaction as his jaws worked at the scant morsels of meat. It took him a while to swallow everything, except for what he spat out one by one into the bowl on the table. Nick counted four *tinks* of something hard against the metal. He peered over the edge of the bunk and saw that they were claws.

The soldier offered a foot to the woman, and then the sounds of two people crunching through bone filled the compartment. They washed everything down with an unidentifiable pink soft drink, after which the man gave a loud, contented belch and she rolled her eyes.

Quietly, without fuss, the soldier offered each dish to Nick, who began to take small amounts of everything—salted fish, fried bread rolls, a purple stalk of sugarcane, candied lotus roots like cross-sections of something lacey and beautiful that had grown on the bottom of the Yellow Sea. Smoky sausages, plum candies—the banquet was more than Nick could have hoped for, and none of its myriad flavors was familiar to his tongue. That seemed important just then, hanging half-on half-off the top bunk, peering down at that sweaty round head and joining this feast. When the train stopped briefly in Zhangjiakou, the man slid the window up, barked an odd cry, and a handful of boiled black-veined goose eggs—not the kind containing embryos, Nick was glad to see—was thrust at him by a woman on the platform. He gave the first one to Nick. The egg had been boiled in black tea, and Nick realized that it was the most delicious egg he'd ever eaten. He also realized that his stomach was taut. Lying on it shortened his breath into perplexed little gasps.

The woman wiped her mouth and returned to her reading, but the man kept at it, smacking and munching for another thirty minutes. He worked through several false endings, during which he listed on the bunk, grunted, gasped and massaged his thighs, before plunging back in. But no matter his capacity, eventually he, too, wiped his mouth. This was the signal for the woman to tuck her legs under the blanket, and, to Nick's surprise, put her feet in the man's lap. Contented, he picked his teeth with a matchstick.

Nick rested on his back beneath the flickering yellow bulb. Although his pack made a good pillow and the hour was approaching two in the morning, sleep eluded him, and he felt a childlike urge to stay up. The soldiers showed no signs of fatigue; their occasional, quiet exchanges were soothing and so different than the language he'd gotten used to hearing as he moved through vast, weedy courtyards and through homely alleys filled with children. Kilometers passed. From somewhere toward the front, the train was gasping, but even this was nothing but the heavy, regular breath of a sturdy pack animal that knows well its way home.

Then the soldier called out.

At first Nick thought it was to his partner, but the soldier was in fact addressing him, repeating the same word over and over and pointing at himself.

"Mingquan," he said again.

Nick shrugged blankly, his mind fogged by the hours of travel, and the man tried another tack. Pointing first at the woman, he said, "Rong," then back at his chest, "Mingquan."

It clicked suddenly and Nick felt stupid. He nodded and pointed to his own chest, imitating Mingquan's gesture. "Nick."

"Neek."

"Yes, Neek."

Mingquan and Nick nodded sagely at each other while Rong continued to read. After a minute spent absorbed in gentle, mutual nodding, it became apparent that Mingquan knew as much English as Nick knew Mandarin, which was, practically speaking, none. But it was okay, because, drawing once again upon his bottomless tote, Mingquan produced three aluminum cups and an unlabeled container the size of a wine bottle filled with a clear fluid. There was no doubt that it was homemade. He winked at Nick and earned another roll of Rong's eyes for the effort—she seemed to watch everything that went on around her, even though she rarely appeared to lift her gaze from the pages of the magazine. After diligently wiping one of the cups on his spotless white shirt, he waited until Nick crawled from the upper bunk on his side, stepping apologetically onto the edge of Rong's bed before dropping to the floor. She didn't seem to mind, and Nick took a place on the edge of the lower bunk opposite the soldiers.

The liquid tasted strange, a curious mix of fermented corn and maybe juniper, Nick couldn't be sure. He sipped gingerly, thinking it was a little like mixing whisky and gin. Rong swallowed her dose without a grimace, but shook her head when Mingquan, who had opted to deal with the heat of the drink by not allowing it to touch the sides of his throat, motioned to refill her glass. He shrugged and poured again. Soon, a spreading warmth began in Nick's torso and migrated outward into his extremities. His legs felt that delicious tiredness that came with drink, as though they had melted into the mattress and had fused him to it. One more drink and Nick couldn't stop grinning.

In an instant, Mingquan came down heavily on the bunk beside him, a pack of playing cards in his heavily creased, square palm. He gave Nick a slap on the shoulder and began to deal cards at a suspiciously deliberate pace. As he taught Nick in pantomime a game called *Choi Dai Di*, the contents the bottle gradually diminished, and they grew very drunk and becoming progressively clumsier, dropping hands and slumping against the rocking carriage wall, spurred to great outbreaks of laughter at each other's fumbles. Dozens of hands passed like this, and dozens more with only the deep, regular sound of air being taken in through their noses.

Rong read quietly through it all, and with the drink in his blood, Nick studied her face openly. Suddenly she became a reclining blur, and Nick rubbed his eyes. The image cleared a bit, but it was still akin to peering through very old glass, streaks of age rendering the images teary and already on the way to being forgotten. The color bled out of her hair, from black to dark brown and then to blonde, not the way he remembered her but the way she had appeared after her voyage here; a whisper of Rong's laughter sounded like his wife's whimper. Nick wiped his eyes.

Mingquan slapped his leg sharply, and the woman on the bunk became Rong again. There were two fresh drinks on the table. The bottle was almost empty.

Nick cleared his throat. "Mingquan?"

"Eh?"

"Do you see this?" Nick retrieved the photograph and held it out. Mingquan studied it carefully, touched the corner of his closed eye in approval, and then glanced over at Rong.

"I know. I took this on the day we met. I knew I'd need to remember that day."

A smile.

"Jane was her name. *Is* her name; she isn't dead." Nick shook his head, brows lowered. "She isn't dead," he repeated.

A sip.

"They came here together, on this very train, her and Fiona. 'A simple vacation,' she said, 'don't worry.' I didn't. But when she came home, she said she couldn't be happy with me anymore." He grinned. "Actually, she said that she couldn't be happy without *her*."

A smile.

"I still love her, though. I'm not angry at all. We only get one life. Shouldn't she get to be happy?"

A nod and a smile. A refill for Mingquan's glass, and one for Nick, as well.

"I think she should get to be happy. She was my wife, and I'll always have that."

A nod.

"She was my best friend for almost twenty years. Shouldn't I want what's best for her? Shouldn't I help her to be happy by being happy for her?"

A smile.

"I think she still loves me. I think that."

A nod.

"She wanted to stay friends. I'll have that, at least."

A smile. A nod.

Nick chuckled. "You know what I like about you, Mingquan?"

"Eh?"

"You're always so positive. Look at you! You can't understand a damn word I say, but you're always nodding. Grinning and nodding at everything I say."

A nod.

Nick smiled. "I've thought about killing myself. I should, shouldn't I?"

A sip.

"It would hurt her. I don't want to hurt her."

A nod.

"She has Fiona now. She'd never miss me, would she, Mingquan?"

A sip. Nick waited. Another sip.

The train was gasping harder now; there must have been an incline. Nick imagined it slavering and shuddering up the track a ways, a place that suddenly seemed very far away. Nick swallowed.

"She was my home. I'm just trying to get to know her again."

A nod. A smile. A sip.

Nick fell back against the wall of the compartment, vaguely stunned to realize that he was unable to right himself, weeping with laughter, his neck twisted against the wall of the compartment at a broken angle. With a look that seemed to convey regret that the night was over, Mingquan dropped his hand of cards to the floor but made no move to rise from beside Nick.

Instead, he began to sing.

His voice was a rich silvery baritone that filled the small space, beautiful enough to finally halt Rong's reading. He took the coarse-sounding *putonghua* and shaped it into a simple love song melody. As Nick listened, fading in and out, he considered his happiness at hearing Mingquan's song, and thought maybe he shouldn't be happy here.

There had been nothing for him in Beijing, Nick knew that now. The glimpses of Jane's last weeks in the pretense of being his wife revealed nothing about her at all. No flashes of understanding, no healing on the gray streets of the hutongs. Jane was gone. No matter how he thought on it, he couldn't see how he would surmount that one terrible fact.

But as he drifted through the Chinese nightscape, it was hard to remain grave. His stomach was full of food. His ears were full of song. *After all*, Nick thought, *what had changed?* Nothing. And if Jane wanted to remain friends, he would welcome the chance to stay in her life, and do some of the things that he had always done for her. In his head, she whispered to him; she was singing too.

Mingquan had a one final surprise. He began to sing the song again, this time in a clearly intelligible Pidgin. It wasn't a love song after all, but the words were all the more poignant for his gentle, conscientious accent:

> *Arise, ye who refuse to be slaves!*
> *With our flesh and blood,*
> *let us build our new Great Wall . . .*

Mingquan's eyes were closed, his hands clasped between his knees, and Nick couldn't tell if the words he sang had been memorized by rote, but then Rong gave him a kind smile that answered his question.

> *. . . millions with but one heart,*
> *Braving the enemy's fire, march on!*
> *Braving the enemy's fire.*
> *March on . . .*

Nick lolled beneath the yellow light. It was almost five. The sun would be rising soon, and the train would stop. His eyelids fluttered like the light (or maybe it was the light that was going out and not him) and then closed. Before he fell away, he heard Mingquan again, softly sighing the same pair of words over and over.

"*Tai tai . . . tai tai. . . .*" Over and over again.

Nick peered through the slits of his swollen eyelids and into the gulf between the bunks. Mingquan was sprawled on his back at Rong's feet, his face turned to the dark underside of the berth above. He was absently rubbing his round belly with one hand. The other was tucked behind his head.

"*Tai tai*," he called a few more times, more softly and then followed by sounds of deep sleep.

Nick didn't have to look up the word to know it meant "wife."

At the thought of his own wife in a compartment very like this one—perhaps even this very one—lying in love at her girlfriend's feet, an unexpected peace flooded over him. He closed his eyes and savored it for a while.

The Lion of Fez

Fes el-Bali. The fabled heart of Morocco, where nothing had changed in one thousand years, and nothing would for another thousand or more. Fez the Ancient, where time was irrelevant. Wet stones, broken ground, cracked walls married by impossible angles and cut by niggardly strips of blue sky so far removed from life in this warren that they felt like forgeries, just more bait for the soul.

There was a traveler alone in Fes el-Bali. But not for long.

The boy looked all of eight, but his age probably was closer to thirteen—the traveler knew that a lack of good food and an abundance of cigarettes did amazing things for growing bodies. His clean skin was surprising, as were his brand new sneakers, although they seemed a little loose on his small feet. The traveler, a tall, craggy 44-year-old who knew well, and preferred, the solitary road, towered over the boy, but the boy stared him down, his sharp little face softened by a cheeky grin.

The traveler was unsurprised when the boy addressed him in English.

"You need a guide here, mister! You are now in Fez medina! Fez medina is very dangerous for you, very big and you get lost quick." His rapid-fire speech was startling in its clarity, but the man gave no hint that he had understood. Sometimes it was best to play dumb, he knew, so he replied in broken Arabic, refusing to divulge his identity for the moment. He told the boy he came from Poland, which was true enough by heritage, if not by birth, then unleashed a few quick sentences in that language to buttress his story. Every tout the traveler had ever met in the world knew that Eastern Europeans were one step above the Russians in terms of financial liquidity, and that wasn't saying much at all.

The boy regarded the man with suspicion as he spoke again, in English. "You are not American?" He rubbed the hollow above his little belly absently as he pondered this. "I think you are American."

The man sighed. Feigning a language for six weeks had left him distanced, even from himself. It was an emotional buffer that bothered him. Besides, the boy looked too small to be harmful—tiny fingers wrapped tightly around a bent cigarette—although the potential to be annoying lurked within the amused suspicion of his sun-dried face. "You win, little man. I'm American as Joe DiMaggio. But I don't need a guide. Thanks anyway."

The man began walking again.

"Ten dirhams for one hour!" he called from somewhere behind.

Less than a dollar. "You're no guide. I know better than that."

His little steps quickened until he had drawn beside the man, whose giant stride was cramped by the moldy pathways, which were less like alleys than the spaces between buildings, haphazard bolls and eruptions that didn't allow the walker to maintain a confident pace. Suddenly then, the boy was in front, walking backward, talking and deftly avoiding the veiled shapes that squeezed through the narrow passageway. "I am a *faux* guide!" he declared proudly, thumping his sunken chest with his hand.

The man knew about the legend of the faux guide, hustlers who preyed on the tourists that streamed from the tour buses day in and day out at the medina gates. They had reputations for leading their clients deep within the labyrinthine corridors and alleyways, only to strand them if they didn't cough up exorbitant amounts of baksheesh. That's if the tourists were lucky. If they weren't, they found themselves vigorously beaten and missing their money-belts; every year, a few wanderers simply vanished, slipped between the cracks of these ancient medinas. Faux guide indeed.

The little Arab turned into the impossibly thick clots of figures funneling through a dripping archway up ahead. Plump women, veiled in black, poured through that gaping mouth and clucked like hens as he elbowed them aside. As the boy pushed blindly through the stampede, the man took the opportunity and turned sharply down a side street, almost enjoying the game and laughing to himself as he imagined the boy's dismay when next he turned around. With the crowds as they were, it could be a while. A *long* while.

The man was still smiling a few minutes later when he heard the sound of rapid footfalls behind him, heard the voice ring out like nothing had happened, as if perhaps he had turned down the alley and had forgotten to call out to him by mistake.

"So, ten dirhams. I will take you to the tanneries."

The man ignored him. A beggar squatted

up ahead, just outside the stream of foot traffic. His face was buried in one hand, the other outstretched, motionless as a bog mummy.

The man had traveled much of the world, and he tried to be respectful of the customs wherever they went. *Nop* the Laotians, keep your soles down in Indonesia. Never make the OK sign in Brazil unless of course you want the recipient to either howl with laughter or pull off your shirt. The traveler knew that one of the five pillars of Islam was the giving of alms, so as he approached the beggar, he dropped a one-dirham coin in his palm. It bounced from the callused flesh before he could close his arthritic fingers around the silver piece, onto the ground and then into the hip pocket of the faux guide.

"Give that to him," the man said, but there was no heart in it. It seemed futile here. The constant barrage of vendors and touts, beggars and hashish dealers, had seen to that. "What kind of Muslim are you, taking money from a beggar?" he asked the boy instead.

"I am a poor *Meslem*!" He looked up with a grin as the traveler fished for another dirham to give the beggar, who was peering into the creases of his palm uncomprehendingly. The beggar's skin had the texture of the crust at the bottom of a loaf of *khoubz*, but the traveler held the coin there until he felt the scrape of calloused fingertips closing.

Alms thus given, he spun down the first alleyway that caught his attention, and the next one after that, always with the swiftly fading hope that the boy would either become separated from him or lose interest. He did neither, but the man did succeed in inadvertently letting the medina swallow him without a trace.

The acrid-sweet smell of something dead hit the man's nose, wafting from the black gap between two grubby stucco buildings that leaned toward each other like drunken old men. He turned away from it, heading back the way he'd come, when he noticed two other boys had approached the faux guide. He whispered something to them and they bolted past the man, into the alley from which the stench emanated. Maybe he had sent them away—*beat it, chaps, this one's mine.* Then another thought seeped into the din pressing upon the man, a dark rider atop the back of the first: Maybe he had sent them to get some older friends to roll the stupid *ferengi* that had wandered so deep into such forbidding territory.

No matter his motivation, the boy didn't reckon on the traveler's compass, which he now whipped out with a flourish. "I have no camera.

I have no money. No passport. No Carte credite. I left everything in my hotel. The only thing I have—" He thrust the compass in the boy's face, who winced as though expecting a blow, "is this. And it will do your job just fine. *Ma'a salama.*"

The man had come from the north, and now he headed in that direction. Of course, in this warren, the streets often dead-ended or wound any which way but straight, but he tried to keep to that general heading. Soon, he came out onto a wider street, at least wider than the ones through which he had been hurrying. Shops lined either side, a thousand points of glinting metal that winked by as he passed through the brass makers' souq. Cajoling voices brutalizing English, *just come for a look.* Dark eyes in dark places, watching.

The man's cunning plan with the compass fell apart when he finally reached the North Wall because the alley disappeared into it, terminating at an old ceramic absolution fountain laid out with squares of colorful tile. Nervously, he looked left and right, trying to get a sense of which path to take, but both choices veered steeply downslope, away from the wall beyond which he knew were air and light and open spaces. Two cats screamed at each other from somewhere within a moldering alcove. He hurried left.

Cul-de-sacs mocked him, circle lanes tricked him and sucked at the strength in his legs. His back was a palette of dust and sweat. Head down, he kept moving. Lilliputian doorways set in the mud-brick came up to his waist, leaving the impression that the buildings had sunk beneath rippling waves of worn stone. Peering inside irregular openings, he saw long, low rooms lined with straw and packed with clacking looms. Old women worked the looms, and as the traveler looked on, one of them fixed him with impassive eyes. Her face was covered by faded blue tattoos that dripped from the underside of her mouth and ran down her chin.

The man stood. His feet felt numb, but they still carried him, and here, that was enough. Ten paces over broken ground encumbered with heaps of straw and rubble, buzzing insects. Ten paces further, tall buildings made of houses piled on top of houses produced geometry that made his head hurt. The sun couldn't find the cobbles anymore, and the click-clack of the looms rising and bouncing from the leaning walls was suddenly the mad scrabble of chitinous creatures belowground. The man felt logy, as though there were a fist pressed insistently, firmly, against his sternum. His eyes were dry and red.

Then a familiar voice came from beside him, beside him and a little below: "Ten dirhams, no problem. I accept."

The boy had somehow followed the traveler all this way without gaining his attention. Now he looked delighted.

As the African days had passed by during this long sojourn, the traveler had taken on a motto with which any Muslim would agree: If it were written somewhere that something should happen, that he should go somewhere or see something or meet someone, then it would happen with no assistance from him. And if not, well then he'd never know anyway.

Mektoub, it is written. It was the only way to live here. The man sighed. "Five dirhams to Qaraine."

The boy held out his hand, but the traveler shook his head. "After."

The boy trotted back downhill, into the medina. After a final moment spent weighing nonexistent options, the man loped after him. The boy was moving fast, ducking around black corners and into even blacker alleys as though trying to escape a pursuer, occasionally pausing for a beat in a lightless courtyard before skipping ahead over low walls and slipping sideways through crumbled passages.

Ten minutes later, they stood panting
before a pair of wooden doors thrown open and
towering against the merest sliver of sky. Once
again, the boy stuck his palm out, and this time
the man dropped four one-dirham coins into it.
The boy's smile vanished, but the man reminded
him of his earlier thievery. The boy nodded,
slipped the coins in a pocket, and assured the
man he would wait outside, and perhaps show
the way to the tanneries or the water clock for
a couple dirhams more. The man shrugged and
said goodbye to him for a second time, knowing
that it wouldn't be the last.

Drowsy gloom seeped from scattered
recesses of the ancient university, and the endless
repetition of passages from texts by monotone
voices freighted the air like a sour spice. As the
man nosed around the courtyard, he recalled a
foray that had taken place yesterday.

On his first trip here, he'd hired an
official guide sporting a big brass name badge
pinned to a pristine, pointy-hooded djellaba that
he wore over a business suit. He'd been hovering
solicitously near the doors of his hotel and the
traveler had figured that, with 9400 alleys that
made up the old medina in which to become lost,
a guide would be an asset, one that would wring
the most from his brief sojourn and perhaps gift

him with places that were off limits to unescorted visitors.

Always impeccably polite and speaking English better than the traveler himself, the guide had instead taken him to one shop after the other, lingering outside while his friends turned up the pressure to buy armloads of trinkets and crafts—some exquisite and priced to reflect that, others gaudy to the point of embarrassment. The idea was as the traveler's wallet thinned, the official, state-sanctioned guide would feel his billfold swell from the owner's kickback—all this for only 150 dirhams and five hours of his life. Also naturally, the traveler refused to buy a single blue ceramic evil eye, not a hunk of greasy Frankincense. *No, really, I don't feel hungry. Not so thirsty, either. My back is much too sore to carry a life-size statue of Hassan II, but otherwise, I definitely would take it.*

Where at first the guide had walked with measured steps, hands clasped behind his back in a manner that superficially resembled piety, by the time the traveler had finished with him his stride had lengthened alarmingly, and whenever the man paused to speak with a metal-maker unknown to the guide (or at least *unliked* by him; the man had the idea that there were few things that moved here that escaped his guide's knowledge), the guide had discouraged lingering with sudden, sharp coughs in the ear, and devastating sighs each time a question was posed. When the traveler finally demanded to be returned to his hotel, the guide churned through crowds with his hands clenched painfully behind his back, cursing curious mules and the boys who led them, and leaping, froglike, over sleeping forms in the gutter.

Now, amid the quiet sanctuary, the traveler glanced outside the entrance vestibule. The little faux-guide sat on the ground opposite the door, his back against a crate of potatoes. He saw his client looking and made a shooing gesture with his small hand.

No hurry.

Revivified by the Qaraine, the traveler decided to let the boy take him to the tanneries after all, and he skipped ahead as they walked together, dodging left and right to avoid being trampled by melancholy asses carrying cases of cola, black-and-white televisions, piles of bleeding sheep heads, and all of the other elements that constituted life in the Arabic medina. They went together down a main avenue, still far too narrow for a car, but wide enough for medina horses to get along. The boy's voice was filled with patriotic pride as he told the traveler of these horses, bred for centuries for their calm outlook on life, all of which was spent shuffling, head down, through the slimy alleys. After the explanation, he stopped an old man and asked that he show the horse's shoes. Although the horse was loaded with vegetables, he prodded it with his elbow until the animal raised its foot for the man's inspection.

"I'll be damned! He's wearing old tires for shoes," the man exclaimed. After another moment, when he was sure the traveler had seen enough, the boy nodded and the old man lowered the horse's leg.

A roof of thin slats blotted out the sun and cast the path in indigo shades. Hundreds of stalls and tiny shops did a bustling trade, and the scents of food and spice, animals and dung, were wet and heavy on the air. Although not unused to Arabic cities, the strange and displaced sounds in this medina continued to catch the traveler off guard. An argument in mangled French filtered through a lattice below a terrace upon which a dirty lamb paced; the Koranic chant of unseen children was the score for a dying donkey that quivered in an alley as a group of men looked on.

Nearer now to the tanneries and the walls narrowed, stark buildings whose tops touched several stories overhead, balconies draped with moss and spider webs of cracks. The only evidence of the tanneries came when the wind shifted and sent an acrid plume of vat fumes settling into the still air of the alleyway.

The boy ducked through an unmarked doorway and up a flight of stone steps, where there was a windowless corridor, creaking doors, Arabic pop on an unseen radio, and then they stood together on a canted stone balcony, and the traveler was amazed.

The tanning vats were entirely enclosed by low, flat-roofed houses that had grown up around and atop one another with a metastatic disregard for flow and symmetry. Hot air whistled across their faded stucco rooflines and entertained gulls wheeling above hundreds of large stone pits filled mealy stews of animal skins. Under the sun, fifty or sixty shirtless men stomped and flung and slapped the skins, their legs glistening as they clambered from vat to vat. Just below the balcony, another group flayed the skins from piles of dead sheep. From three stories above, it looked as though they were playing in piles of pink cotton candy.

"There is everything in the pits," the guide informed his client. "Piss, pigeon shit too!" he exclaimed, perhaps hoping for a reaction, which he did not get. "Ha! Look at them!" He stuck out a finger.

Across the sinkhole was another tall building, another terrace. Thirty pale men and women milled upon it, arms full of buttery bags and purses purchased only moments ago, and sprigs of mint held tightly beneath their noses. Shutter-slaps and excited voices floated across the gap and broke the traveler's trance. He glanced back and saw his little guide half-hanging over the low stone wall and staring at the hot earth, rapt, watching the men work as though he had never before seen this tableau, even as he had never seen anything else.

"Hey."

The boy straightened.

"Thanks."

"It is my job." He squinted into the sun. "What's your name?"

"Alex."

"You look like Indiana Jones, Alex."

Alex laughed. "And you look like . . . a damn little kid. What's *your* name, then?"

"I am *El Asad* to those who know me. I am the Lion." He once again thumped his sunken chest. "I am the oldest brother of seven—" he began, but the man waved at him for silence. The faux guide sob story always started like that. Alex could have told Asad's own fictional life story better than the boy could have told it himself— he'd heard enough versions of it to know. Maybe this one should begin with how his father had suffered a heart attack or something equally debilitating which forced him into guiding to support his family and aunt (who also lived with them, with her own children) and ending with a suitably tragic beating at the hands of the police. But the Lion was young, and after all, a lion; he could take it for now. Besides, he was doing his family duty, and that was what mattered.

It was always the same.

Slanting light puddled into bloodstains on skins of decaying masonry as they pushed ever deeper into the pulsing gut of the medina. Alex lit a cigarette, exhaling the blue smoke over his shoulder. The pressure of a half-million people cooking, working and beating out a living in an area the approximate size of New York's Central Park settled onto him, but it was a soothing pressure, the hot arm of an old acquaintance on his shoulder. Wood smoke tainted the air and bled into the heady aromas of the spice souq that appeared at a junction of courtyards and closed gates, ground peppers, vinegary sumac powders, star anise, exotic leaves and milled seeds the prizes over which flocks of the veiled hens squabbled.

The cigarette burned down and Alex disposed of it as the locals did—he flicked it on the ground between his feet. Asad went after it faster than the one-dirham coin and managed to take three deep puffs before the filter smoldered between his dark, crooked fingers. He made a happy face to counteract the glare Alex gave him.

"If you need a smoke so bad, ask for one." The agility and nonchalance with which Asad crawled after the dropped cigarette was viscerally disturbing, and something Alex would have preferred not to see again.

"Can I have one?" Asad asked immediately.

Alex flipped one over his shoulder and Asad caught it with a grin. His childlike lunge for it made Alex feel horrible for the thing that he had given him, but lung cancer wasn't a top concern here, of that he felt certain. He lit it for him, and took another for himself.

Occasionally, Alex questioned Asad about buildings that interested him, or for translations of signs or a phrase that might prove useful later, but for the most part they walked in slow silence. He was letting the feel of the place wash over him, letting it invade his pores and his head. Without his help, his feet found a rhythm; his gaze wandered where it would. And that's when he began to feel it here, that wonderful tingle in every nerve ending within his body, that sense of being so terrifically tiny, lost in the expanse of the world. One in five billion; good odds, ones that had always been all right by him.

"Want to take me to . . . where?" The question faded into uncertainty. He stopped moving, and Asad favored him with a squint.

It didn't matter where the traveler went. As long as he went.

"Take me wherever you want."

Asad skipped backward past him, all childish exuberance as he said that he would *guide* Alex to the metal-smiths and then show him a place where they could sit for a while and watch them work. He didn't state the price of his services this time, and Alex didn't ask.

On the way to the metal-smiths, Asad slipped into the mouth of a dark arch. The ever-present gloom of the medina veiled details, but Alex could see that the corridor terminated in a small courtyard. Alex asked him what he wanted.

"I want some water, wait here, okay?"

"Show me."

Asad shrugged, a sign that the man took

to be an affirmation. He followed Asad inside and found himself in the center of a two-story covered courtyard. Unadorned spaces that looked like disused stalls lined the bottom floor. Tumbledown doors hung from broken hinges and dotted the upper section. Boys and teenagers loitered about, backlit by shafts of light made thick with dust motes. Two sickly twins hunched over a game of dominoes, their whispered chatter silenced by the foreigner's presence.

Alex called out an Arabic greeting, his voice unintentionally loud in the musty air. None of them responded. The boys moved slowly—some got to their feet slowly, others sat down slowly—and everything had a neglected, dusty patina, as if time itself had run down here long ago. Asad said something to them and most returned to their preoccupations.

"What is this place?"

"It is a *caravanserai*. In Mohammed's time, it was a traveler hotel. The camels and donkeys go there." He pointed at the spaces on the bottom floor, where cots littered with pathetic human bedding stood instead of animals and straw. "The men slept on the other floor. Now we sleep where we want."

"Who?"

Another shrug. He went into a stall and

pulled out a yellowed plastic bottle. "We sleep down here when it is hot, like now. In winter, the top is better." He tipped his head back and drank deeply from the bottle, finishing most of it in a few gulps.

"Where are your parents? Your eight brothers or sisters, like you were going to tell me about back at the tanneries?"

Asad shook his head, his eyes shiny in the darkness. "It is only my mother, and she lives in Marrakesh." He pronounced it "M'roksh." "I come to Fez because the guiding is better. M'roksh medina is too small. I send her money when I have it."

He tried to brush by Alex, back into the flow of foot-traffic, but Alex stood in his path. "When were you last in Marrakesh?"

Asad looked at Alex as though he had betrayed him. "Two years."

After fixing Asad with his gaze for a second more, Alex moved quietly aside.

Asad's face regained its happy mask once more, and he asked the man if he still wanted to see the metal-smiths. The man shook his head in the half-light of the caravanserai. The traveler's hotel.

"Palais Jamaï, Asad. It's time to leave."

The Palais Jamaï was a last-day-in-Fez-so-what-the-hell splurge, a shameless wallow in granite and marble and imported whisky sipped upon a bed that was a silken altar to opulence. The arctic blast rose shivers from the base of Alex's spine as he brushed past four doormen dressed in red who looked past his soiled clothes and into his white face, and dispensed the smiles he had bought with a sack of greenbacks.

At the elevators, standing before his own sweaty reflection, Alex caught sight of Asad through heavily tinted glass that made it seem as though the air outside was cool and crisp and clean. He was drifting back into the medina, back into another time. The doors of the elevator slid open, and Alex stepped through them.

Alex took a sentry's place on his balcony far above the darkening medina, where night did not descend with grace. It overcame him there, a black bag wiping the stars from the sky and falling like grief onto the old city to suffocate the residents in the still air underneath, even as it rocked them to sleep with false promises of coolness and calm. It left the occupants gasping for breath on nights like this.

Above them, out of reach, Alex sat alone, feet throbbing, lungs overused and tired. But these things he could easily ignore; other things were more difficult. His head crawled with the things he had seen—images painted in black. Sleep wouldn't come, so he sat alone overlooking Fes el-Bali. Although only a centimeter of glass stood between the man and the relief of air conditioning, he found that he needed the heat and the smell of fires for a while longer.

He was awakened an hour before the sun by the muezzin in the minaret of the small mosque below crying out in a hoarse and high voice. He sounded ancient and fearful of his god. Dozens of spires pierced the endless sky—or was it hundreds, or thousands?—and from each of these others joined the first in praise of Allah. Their strains co-mingled and rose and fell in ominous discordance. Within this sound, in that sprawling pit of rubble and humanity, Alex imagined old women working their looms, young men hustling and older men sweeping cobbles, others cutting hair, all turning as one at the sound of the callers, and streaming slowly and silently through nameless, unnamable gaps between the leaning walls, gouges, the cuts of a knife across pallid skin.

The muezzins cried out to God a song that to Alex's ears suddenly alerted the medina to the infidel who even now eavesdropped on their sacred prayer, and Alex became unreasonably afraid to move, to call attention to his sliver of balcony above those alleys. Only when silence fell did Alex slip into his room, chilled to another latitude, or to the highest of elevations. After a moment of thought, he went out into the quiet corridor, and found an abandoned maid's cart. He quickly filled his arms with a dozen milled French soaps, a handful of hotel shampoos, minibar peanuts, a thick white bath towel with the hotel's crimson monogram on the bottom edge. Back in his room, he found some cans of soda in the fridge, and snacks he hadn't opened. These went in the bag, along with a sack of toast-points he'd bought from a street vendor in Meknes two days ago.

He placed a call to the front desk, and waited.

When he emerged from the hotel, he was eager to be Atlantic-bound, his pack hoisted high. Once there, he would join a shared taxi and go south, almost into Mauritania, in search of a small, deserted town uncluttered by crowds, devoid of shops, and find a blue guesthouse, and a horizon that stretched away forever in every direction. No leaning walls. No dung fires. No cluster flies. Open spaces.

Alex stepped from the cloistered peace of the hotel's courtyard and glanced around in time to see Asad leap from the shade of a popcorn vendor's cart. He was grinning broadly beneath his sharp little nose. "What do you want to see this morning, Alex? I can show you anything. Anything at all!"

"How long have you been waiting here?"

Asad shrugged, his bottom lip stuck out to convey that it didn't matter. When Alex pressed the issue, more out of a morbid curiosity than anything else, Asad allowed that it might have been a few hours. He was wearing the same shirt as yesterday.

"I'm leaving."

Asad nodded. "I can guide you to the *gare*. The big station. Ten dirhams, no problem."

Alex shook his head. "I know where the station is." He extended the bulging plastic bag he had prepared that morning. On the way down, Alex had also added five hundred dirhams, five times the official guide's rate from the other day—a little traveling money to go with the train ticket to Marrakesh he'd had the concierge acquire before coming down from his room.

Alex's back ached from the chair in which he had slept, but he grinned and scratched at the stubble on his chin, watching Asad rummage through the bag. He rustled with the plastic and held it to his open mouth, closely so that no one around could see. Then he pulled back, tied the top of the bag closed and screwed up his face.

"Five dirhams, and I will show you the best restaurant in medina for your breakfast! Come!"

Alex shook his head. His pack was heavy on his shoulders, and he felt exposed standing in the street with it. "Goodbye, Lion."

Asad's shoulders rounded, but only for an instant. Then he dove into the medina, the plastic bag flopping frantically at his side. The medina swallowed him up and he was gone.

Lightning

There was a hill above the hamlet of Edelény. It was a long, low hill dotted with beeches, clusters of poppies and cornflowers, stands of reeds where watercourses wound down its sides; in other words it was a hill typical of the countryside that lapped against the Carpathian foothills along Hungary's northern border. Boars, deer, and wild goats made their home among the thicker stands of trees, and what was left of a castle crowned the modest summit like the stump of a blackening, broken-out tooth. A sandy path led up to its thick walls through an almost perfectly straight line of poplars separating the hill from the mud houses and conical charcoal kilns of the gypsies who lived on the outskirts of Edelény. The air around the houses there was thick with the smells of cornsilks and pumpkins, the hides of donkeys, and cooking fires filtering up through yellow straw roofs, but was clear and fresh again by the time one reached the small tower of stones crawling with wild roses—the remains of some child's abandoned fort that guarded a bend in a mimic of the castle, lost among sunflowers with heads as broad as peasant faces.

On a frosted afternoon of 1956, four small, blonde sisters were padding barefoot through the castle's dark corridors, following a tortuous path they knew well. They were from thin, peasant stock, ropy in the arms even at their age, which from youngest to eldest ranged from eight to fourteen; a child every other year. There would undoubtedly have been more of them had their mother not succumbed after the birth of the youngest to a long illness. Like the hill above Edelény, this, too, was typical among the people of the town.

It had been raining most of the day, a steady mist that verged on sleet, but sometime around noon the bellies of the clouds had turned darker, and thunder chased the sisters through echoing chambers as they spun from one empty space to the next, laughing one instant, and then suddenly somber.

"Father will find him, don't worry," Eva, the eldest, told them quietly. Fekete Sandor had left for Budapest two days ago to find Peti, who had gone missing amid the uprising, just one of the many young revolutionaries to emerge from the forge between Russia and Hungary. "We must not lose our faith."

"But didn't he say that it had been the students at Peti's school that had started the whole affair?" Zsuzsa asked. She was the second youngest, and questioned everything to the point of annoyance. "Them and the Csepel boys." Csepel was the heart of communism in Budapest, and the workers of Csepel once its strongest bastion, so she said the name softly, but then realized the significance of the revolution beginning there. "I hope the Americans come soon."

Eva nodded. "They will, don't worry." In her head, her father spoke, and she repeated it for the benefit of the younger girls. "Let me worry for you."

"Peti is most likely dead," Marika declared, her voice loud and insistent. Two of her sisters gaped at the thought, which had crossed their minds too often as it was; Anniko slapped Marika on the arm as hard as she could manage. Marika winced and bit her lip.

"Why do you always say such things?" Eva scolded. But there was nothing she could add to take the truth from her sister's words. Radio Freedom had been on day and night all through Edelény the past week, and she had listened with her father to anonymous boys Peti's age first whisper of the corpses of AVO traitors that hung upside down from trees like rotting fruit. Now that her father had made the terrible choice to go to the capital and bring back his son, or worse yet, to join him in a father's futile effort to protect him, Eva thought it best to leave the radio silent in the presence of the younger girls, but she tuned in late in the evenings when the reception seemed a little stronger, and the voices were a little more hushed. Still, the things she heard made her add more wood to the stove, and be glad of her decision. The night before had been the worst—after the Hungarians had ejected the Russians from Budapest and experienced the first real freedom many had ever known, the Russians were returning like a red tide: *At the moment, there is silence, but it may be the silence before the storm. We have almost no weapons, only light machine guns, long-rifles and some carbines. We haven't any kind of heavy gun.*

Eva could well imagine the anonymous young man, handsome like the boys of all revolutions, curls of damp hair in his eyes, the air in his makeshift office thick with sulfur and cigarette smoke as he continued calling out his reports, the pages shaking in his hands. Knowing his fate was sealed. He remained nameless;

occasionally, a turn of phrase, a rare laugh, and he could have been her brother.

In the silence between his words, Eva could hear the thoughts of the entire country. They deafened her as a cannonade of thunder crashed above their heads. The girls were gathered up on the ramparts now; the sky was green and sick.

The sisters sat a little apart from one another on the edge, their knees drawn up to their chins. Reedy stalks of wild grass and sunflowers whipped back and forth below in the confused wind, and their noses were full of the smell of ozone and clay earth drowned by the torrent.

"I think something is going to happen today," Zsuzsa said then. "Do you feel it, or am I the only one?" It wasn't necessary to be any more specific than that; the sisters had all noticed the oddness of the air inside the echoing chambers and along the crumbling corridors of the old stone castle—a cool touch on the backs of their slender necks, a feeling of incredulity and new freedoms, exhilaration and fear, all underpainted by the threat of the unknown and the absence of their father. It was so much like the feeling that was running through Edelény itself that they had thought nothing of it, but nowhere was it stronger than here. "I heard some people talking about the Voice of America. They keep telling us to fight, that things will be okay." Zsuzsa nodded. "I trust them."

"Trust them all you want. Just show me a soldier from the West here to help, and I'll marry him."

Still, for all of their hope and pessimism, there was something in the air. They all felt it. Zsuzsa looked perplexed and sniffed the wind; Eva was silent and concerned. Anikko was amazed as she held out her arm, along which every hair stood erect. She laughed and pointed at Marika, sitting a little away from them on the very corner of the high wall, her feet dangling over the edge. The hair on Marika's head was lifting, the shorter strands radiating outward like a coppery blonde sunburst against the black clouds rushing towards Budapest above them. She swept the ends lightly with her palms, delighted.

Then she was gone.

Before the lightning bolt enveloped them in a formless white cocoon as though they were fusing with the castle, the sky, the world, each other, it flashed across the backs of their burned, blue eyes, and the sisters had ample time to examine and re-examine it. Missing all of them but one as it slit the sky, the sisters watched as it entered Marika's skull, rolling her eyes back into her head and snapping her jaws open until her tongue came out, her body stiffened into the gnarled shape of a witch. For an instant, she looked as though frozen in brilliant white ice, a golem floating a handspan above the thick stones and bearing only a transient resemblance to their sister. Squinting, the sisters could see her dress flame orange as small, circular fires broke out along the sleeves. She must have made a sound when she hit the wet ground amid the sunflowers below—a surprised rush of air, or at the very least, a thud as she came to rest—but the sisters could hear nothing at all following the thunderclap.

Their cry for their fallen sister was unanimous in its timing as well as its pain, but the clouds rumbled insolently above them and drowned their voices. They ran through the empty rooms of the moldering castle, over the rubble that choked its gate, and found Marika among the stiff stalks of the sunflowers.

Anikko's hands hovered before her, flitting toward her sister and then retreating as though she wanted to pull her upright or to slap her face, but she paused when Eva spoke. Her words were slow and measured so that her sister could read her lips; she wasn't sure if her hearing would ever return. "Anikko, stay away from your sister; don't touch her skin!" She turned to Zsuzsa. "Go into the village. Find the oldest man left behind and bring him."

"Why must he be old?" Zsuzsa immediately countered, the veins on her forehead and temples tight beneath her skin.

"Because elders always know best what to do. Now go!"

Zsuzsa stumbled down the hillside, her vision still split by that jagged band of white. Anikko hugged herself with thin, wet arms and shuddered. "Oh, she's so slow, her feet are like blocks of stone. Poor Marika, look there! There's smoke coming from her ears."

Although Eva couldn't hear her sister's words, she winced at the sight of her sister. The crown of her head, the place where this morning she had carefully coiled her brushed blonde hair around their mother's hairclip, was a charred mass of melted skin and hair. The clip's pretty roses had run together in silver ribbons. The sisters wore shoes only for Sunday services in the small, saintless church in the middle of the village, and so they could see Marika's toenails, burned into blackened flakes on her small, muddy feet. Her hands were bent into claws and her chest hitched, stilled, then convulsed again. Her eyelids fluttered as though she were in a delirium; her mouth made the shapes of foreign vowels.

Anikko stamped her foot and cried, "Why won't she hurry? The lightning is in her! It's *in* her!"

"I know it is," Eva said, and then fell into her customary silence, calm even though she knew Anikko was right. She remembered her grandmother's stories—to stem the bleeding, deep cuts should be packed with cobwebs; a bat nailed to a barn door with wings outstretched will ward away ill fortune—but try as she might, she couldn't remember what had to be done for this.

As the two remaining sisters stood together, hands linked against the faltering wind, Anikko's heart-shaped, worried face was turned down upon their fallen sibling. Eva watched the bottom of the hill, where the poplars were shedding their leaves.

In the absence of sound, Eva was surprised that she could still hear one voice.

The tanks are nearing, and the heavy artillery. We have just had a telephone report that our unit is receiving reinforcements, but it is still too little—we need more. It can't be allowed that people attack tanks with their bare hands. Boys, eight and ten, are laying aluminum pie-plates like mines in the streets and oiling the cobbles on the hills with jam. The plates will confuse the tanks only for a moment, the jam will prevent them from gaining a hill or two, but then what? Earlier, a girl of twelve—I have a sister that age, for God's sake—was crushed attempting to wedge a length of steel pipe into the treads of a T-34. What is the United Nations doing? What is America doing? Where are they?

Anikko leaped against Eva, and Eva opened her eyes, which had fallen closed. "Look!"

Zsuzsa was trudging up the hill. She was accompanied by a very old man from the village. Something about his gait made it appear as though his feet were attached at odd angles to his legs, and all along the sandy path, he used the much smaller girl's shoulder for support as they made a slow way up the path toward them. His hair—the white flyaway of an ancient gypsy—twisted in streamers behind him. One hand was clenched into a knobby, arthritic fist. The other hand carried a spade.

When they came to where the sisters stood, Zsuzsa slipped from beneath the old gypsy's cordwood arm and hid behind Eva, who regarded the old man warily. "Can you help her?" Eva asked him.

The old gypsy stroked his chin, which

was cleaved by a deep crevasse filled with cottony white stubble. He examined Marika from a safe distance, one step forward, then one back, as though timing some invisible pulse to which he dared not get too close. Satisfied by whatever he had divined, he held out the spade.

"You must bury her."

Eva held out her hand. "I'm afraid you misunderstood, my lord. She isn't dead. She needs help."

Before the gypsy could respond, Anikko leapt at him, and it was only Eva's quick hand on her upper arm that kept her from throwing herself bodily against the old man. "How dare you suggest such a thing, you filthy old gypsy! You're lucky to remember where you put your teeth in the morning! I bet you stole that shovel, too!"

He nodded as though he understood her type of anger well. "The electricity must be given a clear path to leave her body. Nothing allows it to flow like God's own soil. So you must bury her, otherwise the lightning cannot escape, and she will slowly die." He smiled at Anikko, careful to show her the gray teeth that crowded his mouth in two precise and straight rows. "It is the only way."

Before Anikko could leap at him again,

a group of grubby black-haired children boiled up the hill, gypsy children with mouths running and noses dripping from early winter sicknesses. As they formed a circle around the blonde sisters, a young woman holding her baby and wearing a tragic expression and clucking her tongue came to stand among them. A pair of teenaged girls came next, followed by another old man, then another, then another. In no time at all, the sisters were surrounded by twenty or more people—the dwellers of the mud houses at the bottom of the hill. Although many of them wept openly at the tableau unfolding before them, no one touched the girls.

A current of excitement filled the gathering, although that was only partly due to the tragedy before them. Conversations that had begun down in the village, on cobbled street corners or over charcoal fires, re-formed: *Yes, I know. They were tossed from the windows, every last man. What a miracle—the AVO cannot fly. When do they expect the main force of Russians will come? Already?* Istenem, *Budapest will be torn apart. Where are the Americans? All the boys are fighting—there is hardly a young man left in the village—they will surely kill them all. . . .*

The old man ignored them and extended the spade once again. "The grave must be dug by a blood relative. It is the only way," he repeated, nodding in agreement of himself.

"Don't listen to him!" Anikko cried out again, "He doesn't know anything. He's a stupid gypsy! You should be fighting the Russians like our brother, you coward!"

He smiled. "We gypsies are not concerned by revolutions, because for us nothing will change." A shudder passed through the spade. "This is the only way."

"It is the only way," said the round-faced woman who had elbowed her way to the front of the mass of milling people. "It is the only way," said a nervous, pallid man whose complexion made him appear as though it was he who was destined for the grave that would soon take shape. "It is the only way," intoned a young boy Anikko's age, although he was only parroting his elder's words.

The old gypsy was still holding out his spade.

Zsuzsa squeezed her eyes closed, and to be doubly sure, she buried her face in the crook of an arm. Anikko looked as though she would begin to wail at any moment, as much from frustration and anger as from fear. Marika looked as though she were already dead. Eva took the spade.

She began to dig. It was the only way.

Brothers and sisters, it has come through from Radio Free Europe and the Voice of America that there will be no help forthcoming. With their encouragement and innuendoes they have sent this nation and us to our deaths. A contingent of the Tigers of the Revolution, an offshoot of the Freedom Fighters—city boys aged eight to twelve—have armed themselves with homemade bombs. They plan to run under the tanks as they enter the city and detonate themselves. Dear God, is this what we have come to?

Eva struck at the earth with a widow's grim strength, her blonde curls hanging like fish in her eyes. It was slow work. The ground was clayey and lay heavy on the blade of the spade, which was dulled by decades of pauper's service. Once pulled from below, each load had to be dislodged with a sharp blow against the side of the growing hole. A crone, her head covered by a yellow and black scarf, wept silently and crossed herself as the trench took shape, coming slowly to resemble what it likely would end up being. Zsuzsa held tightly to Anikko. The clouds rubbed each other and whispered strangely.

Anikko tried again, tearing free of her sister with the curled-lip growl of an enraged, albeit small, dog. "Eva, please don't do this!" She grabbed Eva's arm and held tightly to it, preventing her from digging. Her eyes were huge and burned with the strength of her plea. "We've already lost Peti. Maybe Papa, too."

Eva forced a smile. "That isn't true, Anikko. And I've heard of this treatment. Grandmother told me of something like this when I was your age. This might have been what she said."

As she hacked into the soil once again, there came a tremendous crack from very nearby and above, and the grubby people rushed away to find shelter, leaving the sisters alone. It didn't matter; before the thunder could settle into the hills, the hole was done, a shallow rectangle cut into the black clay of the hillside. It was approximately three feet by two feet, and two feet deep at its lowest point, where a puddle of silty water shivered. Marika would have to be folded into the earth, but Eva thought that it was sufficient to hold her body.

Thirty minutes had passed since Marika had been struck, and there wasn't a moment to spare. Her eyes were half-open and she was breathing, but now a new, rhythmic shudder was settling into her joints, as though she kept catching sight of something terrifying and approaching in the clouds above. Her teeth chattered, and then clenched.

Eva rested only a moment before

standing over Marika, moving carefully so as not to touch her. The old man who had brought the spade nodded grimly from the base of the hill where he stood beneath the poplars, taking shelter from the threatening sky under the tallest one he could find—everyone knew that a tree grown tall and unmarred by past lightning strikes was a lucky one. Eva met his eyes and then turned toward her fallen sibling.

Eva studied her sister's dress. It was a long, white dress with red embroidered piping along the sleeves, now speckled with those curious circular scorch marks. Settling her hands on the strong seams along the bottom hem, she threw her weight back against the material, but Marika seemed poured of that black earth beneath her, and Eva lost her grip. Her fingernails raked the wet fabric, bending back until they broke. Seeing Eva's grimace of pain, a look of dismay and growing fear, Zsuzsa abandoned Anikko and took hold of Marika's sleeves. Anikko turned her back to them, partly in anger and partly in fear, but Eva and Zsuzsa ignored her and working together, they heaved at Marika until she slumped into the ground.

"We must put something over her face," Eva called to her sisters. Anna picked up her scarf from where it had fallen, and laid it over her sister's mouth and eyes, gently, like a shroud. Marika's eyes bulged beneath the thin silky fabric.

The sisters held their collective breath as the earth covered the motionless girl's body, all but for a tiny circle of her face. Once done, their shoulder's slumped as one.

Together they watched the ground.

The young man from the radio whispered in Eva's ear as she watched the ground—*I am running to the window in the next room to shoot, but I'll be back if there is anything new. Sending kisses. We are well and fighting at 1320, CET, 4 November 1956.*

GOAT TREES

Dying is: one hundred eighteen degrees in the shade; a creeping nausea; a lung-searing blast through a window flung open onto scalding corrugations of earth high enough to block the view but not the white hole punched into the blue cloth directly overhead; a buzzing in the head; a cauldron of mirages, and blurred blue tearing eyes. Her tearing eyes.

These are the things I clearly remembered. Everything else was gone.

We'd stopped for fuel in some nameless Moroccan outpost only two hours ago, but the memory of it already felt vague, as though it had occurred in another's life. I had closed my eyes as the pot-bellied attendant filled the tank right to the top with *super sans plomb*, sick now as much from the reality of my decision to abandon the coast and head inland as from the heat—the western edge of the Sahara isn't at its most hospitable in late July. But this was to be no ordinary honeymoon—that much I had promised my new wife after discovering that she could be contented by nothing more than weeks spent supine beneath a beach umbrella; for me, another day at Agadir was unthinkable. When the idea of renting a car and escaping the crowds along the Atlantic coast had come up, the promise of solitude had been impossible to ignore.

Now we were cutting the belly of the country, three hundred miles from left to right, aiming for a nightfall in Zagora, the date-palm oasis near the Algerian border where I hoped we might ditch the car and join the small, guided groups of travelers that left north from there from time to time by camel caravan. Moving at night and resting under heavy woolen tents during the day, we'd creep ever closer to the ruins of the ancient city of Sijilmassa. After that, who knew, but this was an outing I was proud of having found. Besides, wherever we went, it wouldn't be Agadir, and that was enough for me.

But that was hours ago, and now I had to wonder whether I had made the right choice, for there was no doubt left in Alison's resolute gaze that it had been my choice to make. And there was also no doubt that I had been wrong. But give me shade and rest and cold water—give me Zagora—and I was sure we'd be ourselves again.

There came a sudden noise, and I glanced up to see Alison looking queerly at me. "Hey? Should we turn around?"

A battered green "Elf Lubrificant" banner slapped languidly against its lanyard and laundry fluttered from a windowsill on the second floor of the tumbledown station. The smell of old motor oil and gasoline pervaded the car and watered my nose. Small noises, metallic clicks, and the groan of springs, and then the attendant rapped on the doorframe, smiling through an expansive beard and wiping a hand across his forehead. Alison handed him a fistful of coins while I drank a bottle of water—a full two liters, hot and flat. Out here, water was more necessary than air, and the plastic-tasting liquid sluiced down my throat without a gasp to interrupt it.

She turned back to me. "We could be on the beach in a few hours. . . ."

"Let's keep going."

Alison didn't waste any time once she heard the click of the gas-cap, turning across the oncoming lane without checking for traffic—there was little movement this time of day. In seconds, the gas station and its attendant were specks in our mirrors as we took once more to the cracked half-lane that passed for a highway here.

Miles went by. Our conversation, what

little there was, turned as fly-blown as the animal corpses that dotted the landscape.

"Slow down! There's no rush, Alison."

"Of course not. You're just dying."

"Don't be stupid. I'm not dying."

"I suppose you're just thirsty."

"That's right," I said, when in fact I wasn't thirsty at all. I hadn't been thirsty for an hour. "Just keep to the center of the road."

"It's not like there's anyone else stupid enough to be driving this way."

"We're halfway there."

"Almost."

"That's what I said."

I rested my head against my arm. My focus grew weak. Freed from the hypnosis of the straight road, my eyes wandered through a surreal conglomerate landscape of the real, the imaginary, and whatever existed between. An ostrich-like bird sat beside the road, its garbage-bag body baking in the sun; a lone figure walked (or was he floating?) through the wasteland, clutching a bottle and nothing else. Smears of green in the haze. It was endless. My eyelids grew thick. My wife kept driving. Lolling in the front seat, I watched her at times from the corners of my red eyes. I saw her skinny arms reaching through the sharp light as though she wanted nothing more than to strangle the wheel; the long, white stalk of her neck was no wider than my bicep. Wife. I rolled the word thickly on my tongue. Wife. Second wife, three weeks into it. A hell of a honeymoon. My face was turned to the open window and the invisible torrent just beyond it.

Outside it was an earthly landscape no more. The wire of the antenna whipped itself into alien shapes and beat strange patterns against the roof of the car. The curve of the horizon was swaying and swelling, bloating and collapsing, as I shrank like a pale insect from the sun coming through the windows. Arab conversations replayed themselves in my head, radios blared. Oceans appeared beside the road, then evaporated into scalding ground. Trees bore massive, hairy fruit.

These last resolved from the shivering air, sparsely spaced but stretching into impossible distances, bracketed by a horizon of wind-scoured rock, and I brought my head up from the rest. I blinked. The fruit of one of the larger trees moved, its long black and white hairs streaming in the wind. We were almost past them, and I jerked upright.

"Stop the car!" I exclaimed, mildly surprised that the words came out as a hoarse whisper.

Alison jammed on the brakes, her eyes wide. Once all forward motion had bled away, she examined me. "Are you going to be sick?"

Maybe, but that wasn't it. I clambered from the car and stood for a moment regaining my legs amid the weeds that grew in great clumps through cracks in the pocked surface of the road. I took some steps; the ground stilled and I wasn't as unsteady, moving slowly toward the trees—the ones with the shaggy fruit—along the right side of the road. They looked so much like a fever dream that I almost believed they were. My forehead burned, so it was possible. But no matter how I rubbed my eyes or shook my head, they refused to wink out.

"Where are you going? We have to get to Zagora!" Alison cried, the violence of heat stealing the strength from her words. She sounded like a child, and I wanted to laugh.

"C'mon, let's go see. . . ."

"Stop it! This is what I was talking about!"

"Can't you see them?"

Alison didn't look where I pointed, instead taking two bottles of water under her arms and cursing softly, as a mother might when her child escapes her grip. She kept her eyes down as we moved away from the road, stumbling over the rough ground like a pair of drunks. Her steps were small and tentative, as though she loathed putting too much distance between us and the little Fiat, which we left where it had skidded to a halt in the center of the single lane. As I took her hand, I saw that she was on the verge of tears. But I wasn't deterred. We passed into a gully, wide and flat, which obscured the trees from view, and there was only the sound of our steps and the papery hiss of air from between our lips, carrying with it moisture that we would soon have to replace.

I began to feel better. Another bottle of hot water and a cessation of the thin but steady stream of carbon monoxide from the Fiat's leaky muffler further quelled the somersaults of my stomach. My vision cleared a little, although when ground crested before us like muddy surf, and we clambered up the rise, I wasn't sure I could trust my eyes after all.

Alison looked up at last. Her mouth opened a little, then closed, then opened, chewing silent words. In the end, she only managed one. "Goats?"

The branches of the tree were creaking with goats—*freighted* with goats. It was their scruffy hides that drew the shadows on the ground, not the few remaining leaves the animals had spared. The heaviness of musk settled over us, and I stifled a cough.

"What the hell are they doing?" Alison whispered. Her eyes were dry now, all of her troubles forgotten.

I squinted into the branches, but such a quantity of these animals so bent on ascending to the shakiest of branches, some only the thickness of my thumb, for no particularly compelling reason stole my words and replaced them with strange syllables and stunned groans.

"They must be eating something," Alison declared.

I shook my head. "There aren't any leaves up there. They want to get off the ground, I think. For shade maybe?"

"They're the ones making the shade. I think they're eating something. Look, that one's chewing." She pointed at a goat above her.

"No he isn't," I asserted, and she fell quiet. An oven-wind blew over us and I held up a hand to shield my eyes. Nothing was moving out here. I held my breath for a beat. The scrabble of airborne grit and the creaking of the goat trees were the only sounds.

"How do you suppose they get down?" Alison asked. She had moved away from the shade and was peering at the nearest animal, staring up and into its eyes. The goat reflected her gaze through his calm, horizontal pupils, as if to say, *Why would I want to do such a thing?*

Not all of the trees held goats, but most did, and the tallest of them rose two-dozen feet above a baked brown hardpan that must have shed water like a sidewalk, and the gnarled branches had carried the goats every inch of that. Even from such close proximity, it was easy to see why my mind had been tricked; some all black, others all white, yet others half-and half, they looked like ripening fruit. Their stillness—utterly free of twitches, lurches and other normal adjustments made for the sake of balance—unnerved me. Although there were scattered goat trees to the horizon and, I'm quite sure, beyond, I had yet to observe them move at all, up or down.

My wife was facing the hot wind, her mouth pulled into a smile as she squinted eye-level at a goat. Wife, I thought again, the word softer and more hopeful this time. I took her by the shoulders. My mouth was hot and dry against her lips, but she didn't seem to mind. She touched my face as I drew slightly away. "I've heard about this, Alison," I said. "These trees were planted years ago from the eldest goats in each herd. They're not much to see in early spring, but by late summer—early autumn, tops—all these goats will ripen to a rich, tender black and fall to the ground like giant avocados. Nature's miracle."

After a moment to clarify that muddle in her overheated head, Alison broke out in laughter.

"Should we shake down a couple for ourselves?" she asked, giggling. "We can plant them in the backyard at home."

The goats turned on her as one, each head homing unerringly on the sound of her voice. She laughed harder, and the goats looked smug. Maybe that was just due to their lofty perches, from which they could naturally look down on us. But I wouldn't have bet on it.

Our earlier tension gone, I rested for a while in the goat-shade while my wife wandered between the goat trees, occasionally singling out certain individuals for scrutiny. My headache eased, and we didn't speak, as though the sound of idle talk might cause this tenuous reality—goats and peace in the desert—to cease. The small camera that my wife had carried everywhere for the past three weeks remained forgotten and silent.

I nodded when she suggested that we go. Zagora was six hours away. We were halfway back to the car when she grasped my arm, hard.

Up ahead, a figure slouched insolently against the Fiat. His pants were baggy and black, and his head was wrapped almost entirely in black cloth. In his hand he held a long, wooden staff, which he slapped on the surface of the road. The tip came down again as we watched. A second later the sound came to us . . . *Thwack!*

"Where the hell did he come from?" Her question emerged as a sharpened whisper. I shook my head. No car had brought him, I could see no houses nearby from which he could have emerged. Yet there he stood. Hidden among the trees, he had probably been watching us the entire time. Now he was waiting. For what, I couldn't imagine. Or rather, I could, and that was what troubled me.

It was impossible to discern anything about him from this distance, and he seemed to have thought the same about us because he straightened and came forward then, poking the earth aggressively with the staff on alternating steps. He moved surely in his sandals, and in a minute stood before us.

I tried to read his intentions from the lines on his face, but the only parts of it left visible were the eyes, dark and sunken into sockets made of craggy skin and protruding bone. They told of nothing but perhaps a hard life. He could have been twenty or fifty.

Unable to introduce us any other way, I smiled. He muttered some perfunctory Arabic *God Be With You*, all the while looking us over. He peered at my watch, my glasses, my pale, pink legs, and muttered something else. Then he stooped over Alison—he was easily four inches taller than I, and she was almost a head shorter even than that—but because of her resolute insistence on local clothes during this trip, something which I had teased her about, only her face was available to examine. The man seemed to approve of her modest linen outfit, and after a long pause, he spoke again.

"N'ta men Amrika?"

Though a little nervous, I nodded. "American."

The cloth covering where his mouth should have been moved, but he didn't; he rocked onto a hip, narrowed his eyes, and blocked the path that led to our car with his staff, as though deciding what to do.

Hoping that he smoked, I pulled a pack of cigarettes from my pocket and offered him one. He didn't expose as much as a glimpse of skin as he pushed the butt between folds of the cloth, lit it slowly with a bright pink plastic lighter, and held out the flame toward me. Though my tongue felt like a strip of beefsteak, I joined him while Alison stood slightly behind me, eyes averted so as not to cause affront. We smoked in silence until only filters remained.

Once done, he thrust against the staff and went to the nearest tree. Reaching up, he plucked something from within the gnarls. When he returned, it was to stand before Alison. He held the fruit in his thick, brown fingers, split it open, and proffered it. The oil filled the creases in his palm like cracked streambeds that haven't seen moisture for years.

"Look, Henry, it's some sort of olive!"

"*Argan.*"

Alison repeated the name of the tree as the goatherd poked at the ovoid seed in his palm and held it so that my wife could see. Smiling shyly, she understood his intent and took the seed carefully, admiring it for a respectful moment before slipping it into a pocket. He nodded and tossed the remaining flesh to the ground. Then he took the camera she carried around her neck.

Plucked it away from her like an argan berry, with thick, dark fingers still stained with juice. He had been so fast and gentle that it took Alison a moment to realize what had happened, now she looked at me with a panicked expression. Meanwhile, the goatherd moved rapidly away, glancing over his shoulder and gesturing for us to stay with a peculiar patting motion of the hand.

I remained motionless, but then Alison nudged me. "That means to follow!" I pursed my lips, and the goatherd made the sign again, as though he were patting a small boy on the head. It didn't look like any such thing to me, but I nodded anyway. "Let's go, then."

As we crossed the same wadi we had earlier, up a small rise, then down again, I whispered to Alison. "What if we just left him, drove off?" My nausea was returning, growing stronger the further along we went after the goatherd. His sandals cracked against his black heels like distant rifle fire, and the wind that took his white linens and thrummed them against his staff made my eyes burn.

Alison wiped her brow. "He'd be insulted. And . . . we'd miss out on something." She gave me a little smile to ease my misgivings, but it only served to point out my helplessness. She touched my forehead with her palm, and winced. "We'd lose our camera."

"We still might," I added, and she didn't say anything to this.

The goatherd was moving much faster than we had been, parallel to the road, but before I could decide whether to call out, he stopped.

We caught up with him only to find yet another argan filled with goats. He motioned for us to stand before it, gesturing with the camera in a manner that could only mean one thing.

"*Photo*?" I ventured. He nodded and the cloth around his mouth moved again.

The goatherd looked the small machine over carefully, giving a desultory wave as I tried to show him the shutter release and earning a quiet laugh from my wife for the act. It sounded nice out here, and I squeezed her shoulder. As we waited for the goatherd to examine the settings and buttons, I couldn't help but wonder why he had brought us here. Although we had passed several trees that seemed on the verge of rending into tinder under the weight of goats, the tree behind us was a small one, and held only a half dozen of the animals. While his attention was diverted, and still posing with an arm around Alison, I took a better look around. Behind the tree, at such an angle that the film must certainly capture it, was a modest house. If we had driven another hundred yards, we couldn't have missed it.

Then it made sense—the goatherd wanted his home to be in the photograph, too. Alison saw what I had, and mouthed the word, *wow*. The goatherd found the shutter on his own time, composed the shot, and took the picture. Then he returned the camera to Alison.

How long has it been since he'd had a visitor? I thought idly. *Did he spend all of the day wandering among these quiet trees, with only his goats for company?*

He must have seen the questions written on my face, because he began speaking rapidly in *Maghribi*, gesturing toward the structure. The barrage of words, Arabic muffled by the heavy cloth, was perfectly comprehensible.

As much as I might have wanted to take up his invitation to join him inside his house for some rest or refreshment, my head was throbbing again. Alison looked as though she wanted to follow the goatherd; she was patting the air by her side she watched my face. Undecided, I faltered, stepped to the tree. Before I realized it, my hand was on one of the goats. His black fur burned my hand, but the old billy didn't flinch at all.

An Autumn Scent

Wood; he smells like trees.

She put her nose to the seam in the stone, and inhaled. Sticky sap, muslin, earthworms. There were other smells seeping from the seam, as well: the hard manly spice of whiskey, a trace of the cigarettes that he smoked, strangely faint. The smell of his pillow early in the morning, the place where he rested his head and the place where she sniffed as long as she was able to resist the urge to run to him as he clanked metal dishes in the kitchen—all competing with the tremendous smell of the lakes that surrounded her, beyond, the big water, and the smell of stone.

He had been in there for a little while now, and she wondered when he would emerge. Concerned, she called out to him, as she had every few minutes for a little while. When he didn't respond—he was angry with her for deserting him, she knew that much—she stood. The northern light was failing, and she moved into the woods to find water before the last of it went.

There was no hurry. Without her friend, she was locked out of the cabin, and she walked slowly, head down and tired, killing time. The thick stands of evergreens were shot through with even denser copses of quaking aspen, and all around, leaves were turning yellow. Their dusty-rug smell cut a very long distance on the edge of the wind. When she came through a deeper pool of the leaves, banked like snowdrifts against the trunks, hiding details beneath them and smoothing out the edges of the world, the smell was one purely of death. The wind through the leaves on the ground here made it sound as though some animal was following always a few steps behind her, following close enough to smell that peculiar spiciness, but just around the bend each time she turned shyly to look. Water chuckled. Something stealthy crept along a tangled deer trail, still far away, but nearing. Insects chewed bark.

The old black dog came to a stop.

Up ahead, there was a small clearing through which ran a stream lined with willows. Further away stood six or seven conifers with double trunks, dumbstruck by lightning. There, among drunken trunks and covered by bowers of branches bending to the coolness of the early night, she drank deeply.

A splash of water wet her short black hair, and she shook her head and laughed. A wave, sneaking up to collapse onto rocks, taller ones marching endlessly in from the big water, and she ran back to the cabin. He was there (he was *there*) sitting in a cane chair on the porch, his smoke on the air, and the scent of leather boots. She ran to him, and he put his hand upon her head.

"Get wet, did you?" he asked her, and she cried out happily, not because she knew what he had said—apart from a few words she could always remember knowing ever since she became, sibilants and plosives failed to create much meaning in her world. She knew no such thing as love; love was too amorphous. All that she knew was repetition and experience—the fullness in her stomach after he fiddled about the kitchen, killing animals for her to eat; the warmth of his hand on her back as she lay curled beside him on their shared bed; the sound of his voice and the smell of his skin.

She tossed her head beneath his touch, and then it was gone. All there was out here was the sharp sourness. She could hear leaves settling, big, heavy hearts sinking through cold air, and when she looked around, she saw that she was alone. All of the leaves still on the branches pointed toward the earth like spades, waxy blackjacks that were the color of campfires during the day but were slowly turning the color of ashes.

These ancient northern woods were thick, forgotten. They were populated only by the most rugged and sturdy of men, men who smelled of liquor and tobacco and the somehow bulbous smell of the green sap of cut trees. The thought of their smells made her realize that they had all smelled like her friend, the one for whom she was waiting, and had been for a little while now. The thought of their smells made her run back to the seam in the stone, run back as fast as she could go. The light was failing, and the sky smelled like snow.

There were holes in the ground around here. They scared her.

Drifts ran between dark, gloomy hills and beneath hollows where the light came through the trees so slanted that even in midsummer it petered out far above the mossy ground. Steep shafts fell away into terrible, odorless depths. In the places where rocks that rolled downhill always smelled of the minerals of blood, the wind rattled through old timbers and turned great wooden wheels atop leaning wooden towers, raising a sound like boars dying. It was this sound that awakened her a little while later.

She sat up and chewed a mouthful of snow. The air was icy and thick with moisture. She squeezed her eyelids together and flopped onto her side. The wood was warm and dry on her fur.

The small craft bobbed and rocked on the big water, and her stomach felt a little odd, like it did after she had been running in circles. His thickly corded arms were flexing, the rod was flexing, and then, far in the distance, she saw a flash of silver rising from the surface of the lake. He gave a gruff cry of joy, and upon hearing his voice, her stomach instantly settled. She leapt into the bow to jump up and down and cheer the action, but the craft was unsteady, and he called out for her to sit, which she did, immediately. After they returned to the cabin, he threw the fish onto the fire until its skin was crackling hot and steaming. He pulled it apart for her, took out the middle bones, and lay the carcass in the metal bowl where she always ate. Oh, the taste of it, so different than when she caught small animals in the woods once in a while for herself.

Her whistling yawn startled her with its lungful of icy air, burning her throat and reminding her that she was unaccustomed to sleeping in the open—her black hair wasn't long enough to keep her warm.

She pushed herself to her feet, shook the snow from her hair, and lowered her head to the stones. They were cold as she put her nose to the seam that ran down the middle. She inhaled once, and again. The hair along her spine bristled, as though she were being stalked.

What was this new sweetness, this unfamiliar odor of sugar? Her stomach rumbled and she made a small sound deep in her throat, cocking her head and wishing that he would come out soon so that they could go plodding together down the tree-hidden path, slowly because her hips creaked and crunched like two trees in a big wind. For a while now, he had borne the smell of advanced age, so it was okay; he was always patient with her because he walked slowly too.

She curled around herself, her nose against her tail, and fell asleep. As she slept, a light dusting of white came to cover her.

For a while, she chased her longstanding foe—a mysterious something that lived in the hollows and hidden spaces of the cabin, something that sounded as though it was perpetually munching its way through the logs or chewing seeds. She could hear her friend laughing hard somewhere behind her and above her as she bounded through the rooms of the cabin happily, skidding around wooden corners as the little something scurried always just ahead of her, just out of reach. It was a sound she wanted above any other.

Her hind legs pedaled in the snow as she ran faster than she had in a long while.

A while later, she awoke.

She listened intently, and heard small animals in the underbrush, both nearby and those half an hour's walk away. She heard cold waves licking the waterline and a bear chuffing from somewhere nearby. There were many bears here, and the woods rang with their growls like thunder. She would fight one to the death if it came to it, but without her friend and his explosive cries and palpable confidence they terrified her. She heard their terrifying *grhu-grhu-grhu* sounds now. They were very near. The noises came and went. He made a sound, one that always went with scratches behind the ears and good things to eat, and she ran to him as he sat by the fireside.

He was tired and quieter than he usually was, maybe because of his age. She was an old woman herself, in many ways the man's true mate, and when she had left him a little while ago, lost in the snow for half a day, it had hurt him. She had smelled it on his skin, on the whiskey on his breath.

Sitting, sunning, by the clearing under the trees, she and her friend sat. The mink was hiding in the tall grass at the edge of the clearing, a low creature watching them, looking for scraps. A growl, a flash of anger, and then came the chase even before she realized it—crashing through the undergrowth, forgetting her age in the heady wake of the mink. Even over her labored breath, she could hear it, hear that it was gasping in terror, and she cried out. On and on they had gone, until she cornered it by the banks of an unfamiliar pond. There, amid a jumble of stones like a forgotten wall, the mink surprised her with a vicious, sneaky attack, sinking its teeth into the dark wet skin of her nose even as it was coiling to launch itself out over the water, where it vanished.

She wandered in a daze through the woods, her nose throbbing, unable to find her way home and eventually falling asleep in a tangle of brush. Then she had heard him crying out for her, and she ran toward the sound of his voice.

By the fire, she bowed her head as he

touched her face. He took her head in his hands, hard, rough even then, and . . . and

She whined louder and then heard his voice from somewhere very distant. She ran back to the seam in the stone and this time instead of her nose, she put her ear to it. She could hear his voice, very faintly.

"Sixteen years you been with me, old girl," he told her, pacing strangely around their den, as though he was trying to find a place to lie down and rest. "I don't know what I'd do if you left me, too."

Sssisssteeen hyeersss. . . . Though she couldn't understand him, it made her nervous, that circling. The sight touched the memories of muscle and bone, and she placed herself in his path to get him to stop. He did, briefly, leaning down to sniff deeply the top of her graying head, pressing his nose against the flat spot between her ears. She tilted her head, quickly, to lick the side of his face, but he was too fast. Her joy died when he straightened, and began his tottering circle-steps once again.

The shadowy wooden rafters dissolved above them, and a handful of early stars peered down between thrown sheets of blue cloud. She had never felt so exposed beneath the sky as she did now. It had so many dimensions,

strata, motions, roilings, and fear stole through
her as she watched it. She sniffed the air again,
perplexed, then lowered her head to the seam
in the stone. It was as though her friend had
been enveloped by something dark, something
that smelled of meat and worms. She pawed at
the ground nervously, whined at the daylight
moon. The smell of the big water was salty and
reminded her of the day of the mink. Then, it had
been the smell of his beard, and of his eyes.

Trees were shedding their leaves on this
still, cooling day, throwing garlands of yellow
atop the old dog as she lay with her nose pressed
to the seam in the hastily arranged flat stones in
the ground.

The midday sky had only strength enough to
glow a dim salmon color, its sun an artifact that
gave away none of its heat. But for the gurgling
hole between two gray rocks, the stream was
frozen solid. There were mounds of snow on
the land, cresting snow along the branches of
the pines, high banks of it creeping up the tree
trunks, tumors of ice hanging beneath the elbows
of the trees. Nothing moved; the world had been
exsanguinated.

A mound of snow smaller than the
rest and piled beside the seam in the stones

shuddered, split down the middle. The plumes of the old dog's breath were ragged, ripped apart by a biting, painful wind as she shook herself and staggered to her feet. She was thin, her black hair matted. The snow around the flat stones was trampled, and there was a shallow, scratched depression that she had made trying to free her friend. Like everything else, it had filled with white.

She put her nose to the seam, puzzled. Unable to comprehend, she stood, fell back into the snow, got up once more. Her rump trembled as numbness formed in the hollow of her stomach, crawled over her, a feeling like when they had walked together far into the forest, a little while ago.

She plodded beside him as he shuffled along, his thick leather boots kicking up dust and gravel like a horse. They came to a steep meadow cut by cold, fast-moving water, and they crossed it; they rounded the shoulder of balding hill. They came to a line of thick trees, and it was there that she saw the mink again, watching them with its tiny black eyes. She stopped walking. Her friend turned to her. His back was to the trees.

She lunged past him without hesitation, throwing herself at the mink, startling it with a tremendous battle cry. Faster than she would have ever believed it could, it whirled into the forest. She plunged after it. Her friend cried out, but she was powerless to heed his call.

The chase was immense, long-ranging. She was blinded by an instinctive rage that she rarely felt these days, a loosening of the joints and a tightening of the belly that made her feel like a younger dog. She would catch the mink this time. She knew that much, and that was all she needed to know. Stretching to slither beneath leaning trunks, scraping along the row of her old, unused teats, then flying downhill, leaping into the mist, over the holes in the ground—those odorless depths—she did just that, pinned it to the soft forest floor, and squeezed.

As she crushed it in her jaws, the woods were filled with the victorious scent of iron. It was a heady odor, and she sniffed deeply, amazed. There was a settling feeling in her gut, a tremor flitting through it as though at any moment her legs might buckle beneath her weight, and then, with a sigh, the ground beneath her gave out.

Down and down she tumbled. The angle of the shaft and the rubble that had collected over a time unimaginable to her saved her from serious injury, but the rough walls cut at her face and tore the hair from her shoulders. An outcrop jabbed her ribs, and she yelped. The mink dropped from her mouth. She struck bottom.

The darkness there was absolute, and there was no sound but for the settling of earth around her, small, quick noises all around her that were like animals approaching. She could smell the dead mink beside her, and she buried her nose beneath her paws, but nothing changed, and so she got to her feet and began to walk.

She walked through echoing chambers and across rushing underground water, through passages where the air was sour with the smell of rusting machinery. She walked through things in her head that were as clear as reflections of clouds in mountain water, and through other things that quickened her steps and constricted her throat. She walked until she thought there was nothing but darkness left in the world, and then the darkness was gone.

When she finally emerged from the drift back into the world of trees, salty waters, snow, and light, joy overcame her, but it fled when she sniffed the air. Nothing was as it should have been. The land sloped the wrong way, and birdsong with which she was familiar was gone. She inhaled again, but it was of no use. Even the sun was unfamiliar in the cup of the valley into which she had emerged.

She wandered alone for longer than

anything she could remember, along bear trails and beside unfamiliar streams, along the sides of distant mountains. By the time she found her way home, and had bounded, crying out, to the cabin door, her friend had hidden himself from her, down beneath the stones. He hadn't come up since.

Something small and brown ran across the path leading to the door of the cabin. Perhaps still scenting the memory of the mink, she caught this creature easily and without thinking. The bones of the mouse crunched and snapped in her mouth, but she hardly tasted it. It was the first thing she had eaten in a while, and it would be gone very soon.

As she chewed, she noticed that this small thing smelled familiar, and she realized suddenly that this was what had been making those noises at night inside the cabin, this little thing living inside the walls that she had joyfully chased around rooms that smelled of onions and old timbers, warm meat and the fire where her friend always sat, his feet stretched out before him, almost in the flames.

She put her nose to the seam. No smell came from it. He had gone somewhere else.

LOVE AMONG THE RUINS

They sat facing one another in the back of the van, four young men and two young women in a ring around a stove. Clouds were pushing in from the northwest, and the crystalline night was turning soft and dull and very cold.

"My name is Yoshio. I have been unable to find work for four months."

"My name is Hiroyuki. I, too, have lost my job."

"My name is Riki. I have been accepted by the University."

"My name is Hozumi. I am a homosexual."

"My name is Akiko. My boyfriend abandoned me."

"My name is Katsu. I am tired of life."

They read their names and simple messages in clockwise order, from small squares of white paper prepared in secret and in advance. The two girls, Akiko and Katsu, sat together, their papers rustling between their fingers. Apart from what they'd just learned, they didn't know each other. None of them had seen one another before this evening.

Riki, hardly more than a boy, opened his mouth to say something at Katsu's declaration, but closed it again. There were rules to follow. They had introduced themselves to the witnesses of their carefully considered fate, and that was enough. They placed their papers in a little stack, and fell silent; there was to be no further talking. Still, as he had opened his mouth to speak, Riki thought that he had seen the ghost of emotion pass over Katsu's heart-shaped face, which was framed by short spikes of black hair and highlighted by the rays of a frozen moon coming through the ragged edges of the approaching clouds. In another moment, the light dimmed, and her face returned to an oval slightly lighter than the surrounding air and containing two glittering places where her eyes were. They seemed to be watching him.

Riki glanced quickly at the others. All were young, all were solemn and strangely beautiful in the darkness, a circle of expressionless faces. The eldest, Yoshio, took up the stove, a small charcoal stove comprised of metal rings covered in soot, a flimsy base, and a grate, also black. He began to adjust the vents on its base with small, feminine fingers, those of an office worker. Riki saw this, as he saw Akiko's short, bitten fingernails; the noose of Hiroyuki's painfully tight necktie; the scars of careful cuts on Hozumi's forearms that were put there during dark hours spent without his lover—or not, Riki had no way of knowing. They had met one another in anonymous white rooms over hundreds of miles of telephone cable, *nomes-de-plume* that over the days had slowly grown closer to their identities, until this night when they for the first and last time gave one another the truth. *My name is Katsu. . . .* Fanciful monikers becoming small, simple names, the names their parents had given them. With the eagerness of youth they had converged on the temple where they had agreed to meet before driving here in Akiko's father's utility van; from beginning to this end, less than a week had passed.

Although he was aware that it might be construed as disrespectful, Riki found himself drawn to study Katsu as she sat on her bare feet, her legs folded beneath her. She wasn't a striking beauty—her nose wasn't very straight, and her chin a little stronger than Riki preferred—but she possessed a dignity that made her appear both much younger and much more wise than the rest of those gathered tonight in the empty cargo van parked atop Shiroyama Hill, just outside the Kyushu Island town of Hiyoshi, overlooking the East China Sea. She may have even been younger than he, which surprised him. He was only eighteen.

Elsewhere on the islands, there were other groups like this one, some smaller and some larger, arranging charcoal briquettes, slumping against each other in red-faced, stoned silence. There were many such temporary clubs, if one knew where to look. In his preparations for his escape, Riki had vetted several, but there had been something about this particular group—their solemnity, he supposed; shouldn't this be a solemn occasion? They were all from around the city of Kagoshima, across the rugged, narrow neck of Japan's southernmost island, so they shared the same sensibilities. They had all stolen cucumbers and tomatoes from the farms along the back roads; they had eaten raw Kagoshima potatoes, juicy as apples. They were a kind of family, destined to grow closer still after tonight. Riki clasped his hands in his lap as Yukio fumbled with the briquettes one of the others had brought.

A light snow began to fall. The air in the van was cold, and silent, shallow breaths hung between them like the pale ghosts of the sins that had driven them into each other's company. Yukio got the stove lit after several unsuccessful tries, and immediately the airtight space filled with a burst of heat. Some of them rubbed their hands together over it in an unconscious gesture of a childhood pleasure; Riki and Katsu sat still. Riki hazarded a glance at Katsu, and thought that she was still watching him.

The snow was turning heavier, but with the addition of the coals glowing beneath the dirty grate, the atmosphere in the van grew thin and light. The stove flickered between them, eating air and giving off the smoky aroma of past meals, slight smells that reminded Riki of summers spent with his brother, Takashi. One Dragon Street had never known a finer summer than their last one, spent with a fervency spurred by the knowledge that Riki was heading for scholarly pursuits, and leaving its cobblestones and ginkgos behind.

That's the problem, though, isn't it? Your brother should have been going where you are to be. Were to be, anyway, if all you cared about wasn't between the covers of old books, that is.

Talking could only breed recidivism, they had all agreed the day before they met, and Riki briefly wondered if the words were an auditory hallucination brought on by the stove. He smiled a little at that—the idea of the stove whispering in his head. What did a stove know? The taste of crabs, the weight of a woman's cooking pot, the feel of spring vegetables against its grate. Riki glanced at Katsu. She was watching him; there was no doubt about that now.

Instead of glancing shyly away again, Riki held her gaze and tried to think of Takashi—leaving him was one of Riki's only regrets. Then it all seemed a little too distant to contemplate, and there was a time when all that could be heard was the occasional crack of briquettes splitting and shifting.

All around, people were wilting. Faces, once troubled, were turning serene. Someone sighed, another cleared his throat. The gang of lines that cut across Yoshio's brow eased, and his face took on the look of a much younger man. Hozumi rested his head against the wall of the van, a smile playing across his lips. Riki imagined that he was bidding farewell to the memory of a beautiful young man.

Suddenly sad, Riki turned back to Katsu. She noticed the motion and fixed him with narrowed eyes. *Why are you doing this?*

Riki didn't know if, inside his head, the question had come from her or was directed at her. A drop of sweat formed in his hair, and ran down the side of his face. The snow had covered up the windows totally now, and the warmth in the van was finally getting into his bones.

I told you. The University—

Yes, you said that already. I know all about that. Why are you doing this?

Same reason as you. It is all I can think to do.

That isn't why I'm doing this.

Katsu raised her eyebrows and yawned. Bored even by the approach of her own death. Riki shook his head.

My brother wants to study books. I just want to read them. Neither of us can, not while I live. My parents haven't the money, and I'm the eldest.

He tried a smile. To his surprise, she returned it. *I like to read books too.*

Who do you love most of all?

She tilted her head. *Nabokov. I love him most of all.*

Then so do I. A wave of lightness lifted Riki from the ground. *What should I do?*

You should take me with you in your thoughts.

It was then that Riki realized that he loved her. It came into his head in a flash, like the heat of the stove on his arms and on his face, suddenly hot as he saw that Katsu's eyes had closed.

His mind began to move faster now, as though shrugging from beneath a great hand. In summers they would sit together in this rugged landscape, their eyes full of the sea, and read in each other's arms in the wintry season.

Her shoulders were turning rounder as the breath went out of her, and her mouth had opened a little as though surprised by a forgotten thought.

They would read Nabokov together. They would take ships to islands and he would never let her grow tired again.

At that, something small and wet rolled from between her closed eyelids. The fathomless black gulf that separated them grew wider and darker by the instant, and then Riki put his hand out and reached into it. He found Katsu's arm. She smiled as though she had been expecting it.

Without words and without relinquishing his soft hold on her lest the break in contact also break their will, Riki guided Katsu to the rear doors of the van. She didn't resist. He slipped her small feet into her shoes before opening one of the doors, she opened the other, and they stepped into the snow.

Behind them, someone pulled the doors closed, but they didn't see whom it had been.

INTERLUDE

There are bees in the jam, she exclaims, watching them with familiar blue eyes, and smiling. *Of course there are*, he thinks, watching her collect fruit in her small hands.

Orange and plump fruit in her small white hands, and she's smiling now at something she's remembering, something they just did or somewhere from where they've just come. More than that, she's laughing at the bees, at their milling fat yellow and black bodies. They lift their stiff wire legs and dart their pike tongues as he pushes them aside with a small sliver spoon to get a mouthful of the sweetness below. *Look, she cries, they don't even care! The bees of Galapagos have found their heaven!* They don't hear her. They bustle and lick their feet as they play in the apricot jam.

Silver trays glint in the evening sunlight, fruits and preserved lemons, olives, smoky shreds of mutton, fresh rounds of bread, piles of sweet dates picked from the creaking *palmeraie* on the other side of these crenellated walls, where among the dark spiny trunks people are falling into sleep on the sand. As the man waits for his wife, a young boy watches. His hooded face is inscrutable beneath hair flaming red and dusty like the sunsets of his land, and yet it holds the untimely knowledge of centuries, of the desert. The boy meets the man's eyes shyly, almost sweetly, but his brown cannot hold fast against such blue and his gaze falters, scrapes over the woman's back, and falls to the tiles at his feet. A small boy looking mysterious and thoughtful and holding a pail the color of lapis, and the man lights a black cigarette and thinks of this place:

Oh, you jewel of Allah—some are unknowable, others slump in stoned blue silence, the red-walled city squeals like a dying thing in the night, but you, you sing to the weary.

He hears this in his head as they walk together through the castle keep, she with her fruit, he with a cup of coffee, a torn piece of bread topped with the bees' jam riding the saucer, and a cigarette in his left hand. Vines chew the stucco with the last of their strength, and it is there, beneath a wall of tumbling bougainvillea, that they sit.

A blessed, untouched oasis, a pompous

man had called this village of broken adobe that instead of a blessing gave the traveler the feeling that the map had run out, and everything here was dead save this walled and fortified oasis; perhaps it, too, is dying, only more slowly. Dust sifts down from the aching blue sky, a never-ending fall of powdered rock smothering the narrow alleys and mud roofs that remind the traveler of Timbuktu even if he's never been.

A light flickers on somewhere, and another. His wife's lips, made sweet and sticky by fruit, purse; her tongue flicks across the corner of her mouth like an animal tasting. She holds out her fork, he eats, he lights another cigarette. There's nothing left to say for the moment, nothing left to do but to watch the maids endlessly arrange low wooden chairs and exhale air scented by spices and dust. A narrow-hipped, sallow girl brings a pot of thick red soup and removes a different pot of soup; a round woman sweeps a walkway with languid pats of the broom.

Yesterday evening fell much as this one falls, and as a hundred thousand have fallen before it—the light coagulating, nothing but sky and sand. Here, entire lives are made of these things. Yesterday, in their small, clean room, they made love, separated from each other only by the grit that lay on their skin. The youth who even now stole glances in their direction wandered past their open window not once but twice, and his studied nonchalance brought giggles from the man's wife.

She selects another fig from a clay plate while he drags a finger across ochre tiles. They turn to brilliant azure and arctic white beneath her touch. He draws a face; his wife draws a heart. Pillars swell into arches that channel the baked breeze into vortices in which twilight swallows play.

As they eat, a man comes to stand before the small, oblong swimming pool that glistens under a dust-raining sky like some obscene sex (for this much water is truly obscene). He is a nameless Arabic prince singing a haunting song of heroism or some forgotten love, a high priest on ecstasy's cusp before the water. The ordinary man, sitting with his wife, thinks:

Oh refuge for us poor refugees running from our lives like so many others, but there are no others here. They all stayed home, and there is no one here but us to hear this royal song.

A refuge, his refuge, like the thoughts of days past when they were younger and in a different land. He tries to recall something sad, and is amazed that he cannot. *Could this be the afterlife?* he wonders. *A place without names.* He glances at his wife as he pulls out of his skin, but she has heard his thoughts and is nodding, caught in the trance of the dream man by the water. The prince's song trails its sacred *sillage*, and on the wall of a dimly lit pink archway the shadow of a maid is dancing with the shadow of a chef. The man's wife sees it, and smiles.

A tall man approaches. The singing prince and the young boy with the pail both watch as he bends from the waist to inform them that their car has been repaired ahead of time should they decide to leave early. Something in the way his lips curl makes the man wonder if this is a suggestion. As the tall man glides away on strangely crooked footsteps as though the balls of his feet were sunburned, the married man follows him with his gaze, not moving his head and not knowing why he feels suddenly that the night has become denser.

The married man asks his wife what they should do, stay or go. *Moonlight guides the traveler in this part of the world.* Traveling by day is hell here, and besides, they're showered and rested, and always packed to go. He finds himself unable to stop nodding in time to the music, wondering why he's been enumerating driving times in his head in the midst of this surreal tableau of bees and immense sky and a young boy watching.

The prince continues to sing. His reedy voice massages the surface of the water into ripples, bringing up the scent of turtles and shattering the face of the waning moon. *Moonlight guides the traveler. . . .* Despite the road ahead, or perhaps because of it, the man doesn't want to swim; he hasn't seen this much water in months, not since anonymous blackrock beaches, the Atlantic driftnet, years ago or so it seems. The married man fears that if he enters, he'll drown.

Somewhere, through thick green fronds bobbing like fat hands in the African twilight, there are bees playing in apricot jam. The man fancies that his ears are full of their sticky footfalls even over the prince's song. They bustle and lick their feet beside the pink archway, where the shadow of a maid still dances with the shadow of a chef.

it is the kind of sweetness
that sticks to small black feet
and it is the time when the light fails
when the loud ones eat
when the loud ones sing
and whatever we sing is a dance
and wherever we put down our feet
there is only more and more
and more the sweet

Mjid closed his eyes. The bees couldn't be helped, but still he cursed them silently. *Saida* seemed to like them, and *Said* Cooke's voice remained gentle, as though recovering from alcohol or heatstoke. Besides, Mjid's mind was elsewhere. After feigning a haughty disdain for weeks, yesterday Ajoul with the round face let him caress the soft place between her legs. His fingertips had carried her glistening warm earth smell as he had lifted them to his nose, touched them lightly to his tongue. As Mjid's thoughts drifted along in Ajoul's cooler waters for a while, he wondered briefly if pale, blonde women tasted the same as Arabic ones. His dirty blue pail swung in his hand, the brown, filmy water sloshing within.

Mjid gazed absently at the foreign woman until he realized with a sudden horror that Said Cooke had been watching him the entire time. The boy was certain that the man could see his every inadequate thought through those pale, blue irises, and his gaze slipped down the woman's body, the sight of which filled him with another swelling of shame, and then to the ground.

Said Cooke. The name, hard and sharp and as anonymous as though Said Cooke were wearing a mask, gave Mjid a shiver. *What kind of man goes around with a surname like Cooke, anyhow?*

Was he ashamed of his father, of his family? Was he ashamed of what he's done?

Driss was singing a song now of the old days of the occupation, and Mjid let his mind drift. *What cool, wet lives they must have,* he thought, *to have such skin.* He wondered what terrible emergency could have deposited them here. Creases too deep for someone his age appeared at the corners of Mjid's eyes as he wondered briefly if he had perhaps seen the couple among the glossy advertisements in the European magazines he sometimes stole to read in secret in the palmeraie, to sniff between the fragrant pages crowded with disgusting and strangely beautiful people. It was possible, he finally allowed, yes, the couple might well be a famous one; he had a difficult time telling Europeans apart. The thought that these were cinema stars watching each other with their pallid eyes brought a shudder to his narrow shoulders.

His thoughts shifted at Abderrahim's appearance from between the screen of vegetation at the south end of the courtyard. He paused, licked his aubergine lips and approached Said Cooke with the mincing steps of a belly dancer. *He thinks he's graceful, walking like that. What a servile dog he is,* Mjid thought, as Abderrahim offered the *ferengi* a moment full of whispered words and a loop of shiny brass keys. Whatever he had said, the man nodded, the woman—at whom the longer Mjid stared, the more disgust he felt; those bony pork shoulders—nodded. He wondered if it would be difficult to touch her, if the opportunity presented itself. He knew there would be none. Foreigners never ventured away from the *ksar* after the sun had set. Even so, people disappeared here; it happened all the time. The wrong *caleche*, an inopportune tire-failure heading toward desert water, a false hitchhiker picked up along a thin road awash with sand—the ways into desert oblivion were many. . . .

Abderrahim's cry of displeasure jolted Mjid from his daydreams. He glanced at the foreigners' table as he adjusted his grip on his bucket. To his surprise, they had vanished, gone perhaps to their room for sleep, perhaps to depart. Perhaps they were rutting again. Mjid debated sauntering toward the guest rooms to see if he could catch them at it when Abderrahim cried out to him again: *I won't say it again, you little pervert: Put the bucket down and go stand beside the food!*

There were no other guests, but Mjid lowered the bucket and ambled to the table to guard the remnants of dinner. On the way, he passed Driss sitting alone on a reed mat, smoking a cigarette in silence, his tie-knot open, sqeezing his temples between his long, cigarette-stained fingers. He didn't look up as Mjid began to flick the bees, one by one, from the apricot jam. Now that Driss was silent, he could hear Aziz, the old chef, chastising his wife in the kitchen as he usually did, his shadow-hands striking and slapping his wife's breast across salmon masonry. Mjid smiled; satisfied by the restoration of order, Abderrahim nodded.

"For Allah's love," he muttered as he shuffled back to his lobby desk, an old pain softening his knees. "No one likes insects in their food."

Exhaust

*Y*ou wish that you had been born into an English childhood. A strange one, that, as far as wishes go. Wet trees, boys and girls prim and respectful, dripping woods full of history and mysteries that had yet to unfold. A strange wish, on the surface at least. After all, you heard the muezzins of the far dusty north of Africa even within your mother's Hungarian womb, amid Bedouin and Berber and strange tall Tuarag nomads dressed in blue, shimmering air and salt riding high upon those broad blue shoulders—one couldn't blame you for wanting a bit of the big wet. The land of Joyce streams of consciousness books Wordsworth and Keats and the Brontë sisters amid the howling ruins of their own imagination. William Blake, won't you meet me down by Bristol, we'll go riding down by Avalon in the countryside of England . . . oh yeah. Oh yeah but you weren't infected there; you were infected among the Arabs watching, a small Ugrian boy who could almost pass for one of them watching with wide black eyes as they loaded the caravans and tugged on the nose-pegs *and disappeared across the sand. And although for the past ten years you've been returning to a small town in Colorado, blue passport in hand, you've never known anything else.*

"Why does it do that?" she asked him as they sat in their shady backyard, sipping coffee and facing each other. "There's hardly a breeze." Her head was covered by an oversized straw hat to protect her Victorian skin; he squinted bare-chested into the bright sky, above limbs swishing like women in long skirts walking slowly overhead.

"Some trees creak, the big, old ones," he said between sips. "Sounds nice, don't you think?"

"It sounds like we're in a ship."

A car engine turned over after a struggle, a lawnmower droned somewhere on the next street. "But I love it here," she said simply then, as she often did, and he nodded. He watched her as she settled into the quietly satisfied state of contemplation with which he had fallen in love so long ago. Four years out of an apartment that had served them well, and then two weeks after her contract with Advanced Logic had expired into a permanent position, they had bought this little home, a house new to them in an old part of town where they slept together under a high plaster ceiling under a wood shingle roof under a creaking honey locust that dwarfed every beneath it.

"Katherine promoted me to travel editor," he said then, and she gasped. It wasn't a theatrical gasp; she wasn't given to theatrics. A small quiet woman, a professional woman, a beautiful woman. His wife.

"I guess you're thrilled?"

He shrugged as a squirrel chattered in the treetop above them. "I never thought I'd see the day."

She knew about his life before her, his feral life—it had been she who had trapped him, rabid snarling lust turning slowly to love under her pale touch, while he waited in Miami for a ship to leave.

"You've got the experience for it." She took his hand across the table, gave a small sigh, smiling with only the corners of her mouth. "Do you remember what you said to me when we first met? When I asked you why you were the way you were?"

He shook his head, feigning ignorance, and she went on, oblivious.

"*The knowledge that I am utterly alone, that no one pines for me anywhere on earth, that there is no place where I am either missed or expected.*

Remember now?" she said, and he had no choice but to nod. "Could you have guessed then that you'd have all this?" She paused, saw something in his face that she misread as contentment. "I'm so proud of you."

On a rude perch of palm branches, a captive falcon, tied by one leg. . . . You like the winter because the cold reminds you of Patagonia, those South American cleavers of granite rising from the sea floor, open ocean and small, wooly horses running beneath a lowered sky. You curse the heat of a late August but you're smiling to yourself at some heatstroke dream. The smell of woodsmoke from your neighbor in the bungalow down the street reminds you of Auckland, clattering birds (the storks of Azhru or Budapest), diesel exhaust in the air that makes your eyes water and your mouth draw into a sly curl (any place in the third world). It's been four years since you tightened the straps on your old drab pack, a small pack that never held more than two shirts, a hat, postcards and tickets and notepads light as feathers. Anything on your back was as light as that, and once three cartons of cigarettes rode you across Russia . . . four years in perfect stillness. Has it really been four years?

Months passed, a morning months later, and he found her holding the bell that had sat on the mantel for as long as they had had a mantel. A thick brass bell, swirling Arabic prayers chasing themselves dizzy around the rim. She rang it sometimes to wake him in the mornings, Saturday mornings because on the weekdays she left before the sun. She rang it to summon him to join her in wakefulness; she rang it when she missed him.

"Where did you get this?" she asked now, for the first time in as long as they had had a mantel.

"An old father gave that to me in Africa. To ward off evil. I could take you sometime."

She pursed her lips as she contemplated this for a moment, before replacing the bell with no greater care than before she had learned where it had been. "Why is it that everything wherever you've been is made to ward off evil? Tell me that and I'll consider it."

That Saturday evening, friends arrived when the darkness came, a strange brew of lanky heavy-lidded hipsters who spoke in verse and crew-cut marketers in oxfords and wingtips with darting eyes. Everyone sat outside under the honey locust, laughing and decrying and opining and drinking and smoking and dancing and dreaming in the suburbs.

Relaxed, resting his head on his arm, he abandoned himself to the infinite sweetness of falling asleep alone on the ground, a stranger among simple rough men, in a nameless desert spot to which he would never return; there was that girl in Morocco, remember? Not a Maghribi but a dusty traveler like you (dust in gorgeous streaks in her curling brown hair), sitting at a deserted café called Patma or Pathama, or something like that. The name doesn't matter; her eyes on your body had mattered, the way they slid upward slowly from the worn sandals, to your tattered pack, to the lines on your tanned young face as she met your eyes and held them in the sweltering Saharan heat, sitting at the Patma or Pathama café like she owned the world. A desert princess who watched you sit for a few breaths wiping the sweat from your face, fidgeting with long fingers as though she were hungry. Travelers are a hungry people, as a general rule. Women both native and far afield hungry people and you loved them all, those intrepid elves and robust mamas and hardcore wanderbuffs with arms made ropy and muscular from years of slinging the pack, very much like the girl at the Pat-Pathama café—that's it, isn't it!—smiling at you as your wife who you wouldn't meet for another two dusty sweaty years slept alone in a college dormitory across the ocean somewhere and would never know the thrill of this, this wonder and smugness of first contact, an exhausted smile returned and then you walked deliberately away from the Pat-Pathama café to vanish into the dead city where an old man would give you a bell in the throes of some kif dream and the girl watched you leave with a puzzled and sad expression. Everyone watched you leave. Everyone you've ever known (except for the one who is sleeping beside you as you dream this) has watched you leave.

He came running up to her as she sat beneath the honey locust in the backyard, a slow red weekend afternoon crawling over the houses and enticing families from dark rooms to emerge blinking pushing strollers and chasing happy dogs along the sidewalk.

He sat down, breathless, and threw a book before her. The breeze was light, and the tree creaked softly overhead.

"I can't believe I forgot about her—you have to read this," he said, and she looked beautiful and coy as she asked him why she should do such a thing, her nonchalance the result of years of such outbursts of exuberance.

"I read something of hers once," he said, laughing, and told his wife of a girl named Isabelle, a European girl who had succumbed to the Algerian lure of limitless distances and the long, dry road. She had left her life to drift wraithlike across the burning ground, nothing but a ghost for the last four of her twenty-seven years, a profoundly melancholic girl who had lived in abject poverty writing stories under skies that killed everything beneath them.

"I didn't even know how close I had come to her. She drowned in the desert, not very far from where I was born." His wife raised her eyebrows and he shrugged. "I guess I've been thinking about her for a while."

"Sounds depressing," she said, flipping the book and skimming the back. "I'm just not interested in a—how can I sum this?—a dead syphilitic chain-smoking alcoholic drug-addicted desert waif's self-imposed suffering." She slid the book away. "I see enough suffering at the office."

He hunched forward. "Try to imagine it. 1901. Her whole family exterminated themselves, one after the other. She was just trying to outrun her fate. Look what she says here—" He showed her where Isabelle had, a hundred years before, written the very thing he had told her back on those rank docks of Miami, *no place where I am either missed or expected.* Word for word, she had said it too.

"Maybe I've been reincarnated as me!" he cried before falling back into the chair with the bewilderment of a degloved puppet. "But I guess you can't outrun your—"

"What would happen if I went off the pill?"

"—fate."

He forgot about Isabelle; the cigarette burned forgotten in the ashtray. A low groan shuddered the corrugated trunk of the locust. "You want to start a family? With *me?*"

She giggled, terrified and thrilled. "I don't see anyone else here, do you? But really, they'll never let me go, and the money is more than enough. And with your editorship, let's not forget that." As the words coiled in air that smelled of grass and fertilizer, clean smells, she realized that she had been babbling, and quieted for a moment before adding, "It would work, you know."

He smiled then at this small, brave woman, and for an instant, he saw her as she would have looked after two months in Cambodia—freckled, her perfect clothes a little grubby, her skin a little rougher but her eyes glowing with the force of her discoveries. He saw the child then, too, a union between olive skin and porcelain, between black eyes and marine ice, six feet four and five feet nothing. It would work; of course it would. She was a perfect wife, her love so overwhelming, a blunt force trauma raining kisses and kindness upon his head. Why shouldn't she be a perfect mother?

"If it's a girl, she had better take after you, that's all I have to say about it."

She flung herself into his lap, her laughing grinning mouth hard against his own.

"I'm taking that as a yes."

"Can I crash in your bed tonight? I don't take up much space, and my money's all gone . . . I've come from Vietnam, oh yeah isn't it sweet? Did you make it down to the Delta?" Two dollars a night to still the clock along black waters' edge—just sleep now.

Storm's coming, second floor.

That's what the man behind the desk of the hotel told them. Oily ball-cap missing teeth in the middle of Nebraska, middle of summer, middle of night. They carried their bags upstairs slowly, moving between paper walls in an unnatural silence.

A four-day road-trip—all that she could take—to visit her sister in Chicago (two fattish kids, chapped hands, downward-plunging lines on her face like gashes or old scars), and now even that was gone and nothing remained of it but the confused sounds of the big smoke in his ears and the knowledge that a fresh pile of manuscripts awaited him upon their return to the small house beneath the honey locust, while his own work, and he along with it, languished.

After his wife filled the tub, he kissed her mouth and went downstairs with a cigarette in his hand, past a rattling fan in the hallway beating heavy air. Outside, in the sky, a giant depression of black—he could feel the weight of the water it contained. Flags were taut and pointing, even the big one at the deserted car dealership across the road, lanyards clicking like rail-ties beneath a rushing train. Black, but he could feel it. A piece of the world had disappeared there, and all that remained was the perfectly steady suck of atmosphere. It seemed as though every molecule from miles away was converging on that one black rend in the sky. He wanted nothing so much as to run toward it, arms above his head, until his feet left the ground for good.

Even out here in the flatlands of Nebraska, leaves are changing, mindless cycles yellow leaves that make you wonder what a yellow leaf looks like in Algiers. The soul no one suspected him of possessing had been exhaled, a murmur of resignation from ancient Islam, in simple harmony with the melancholy of life . . . where did you read that? Some bus stop, you know that much (in a place where I am neither missed or expected). Broken spine torn pages and when you were done savoring the freedom of a brilliant woman's journey toward her torrid, passionate death you gave it to a pregnant girl squatting on the sidewalk and told her in pantomime that this book would change her life but which probably came out as 'I pity you, so here.' Months later, you passed through again and found the very book for sale by a street vendor in a skullcap. While you were examining it for the note you always write in such travel companions that are destined to be lost along the way (I have been here; have you?), he grinned and told you it would change your life.

"Why isn't it working?" she said softly, holding the little wet plastic stick in her white hand. "We've been trying for months."

"*Maktoub, maktoub,* and all of that," he said, smiling, but then the smile faded when he saw that her hand was trembling. Each month she seemed to come a little late, more hopeful than realistic, and she'd run off to get a kit. It was negative tonight, as it always was. "It's Arabic for *if it is written,*" he added quietly.

"But what can be written for us if I can't give you a child?"

He could give her no answer but to take her into his arms and hold her trembling while she cried but only for a little while before pulling free.

"You shouldn't worry so much," he told her. "You shouldn't ever worry."

"Why not?"

"Because you have a good life, a good job, this place this street everything."

"And you," she added softly. "Can we try again tonight?"

Curls of blonde fell across her face in the warm light, stunning him in the warm light. "Are you too busy to try again right now?"

You flip the old guidebooks while she sits earnestly in a blue cubicle across town, trying to remember where you had been when you drew the graphite circles, those happy exclamations in the margin. Messages from the other side of time (you're an idiot if you miss this!!) maybe at the Otel Excelcior overlooking the medina of Dar Al-Beda (don't you dare call it Casablanca or I'll strip you of your traveler status and call you a fucking tourist), yeah, that's the place. Flies and roaches and a stray cat named Ishmael who took a fancy to you as you rested with the casements cranked wide open, listening, rapt.

You practice your Mandarin in Chinatown; you eavesdrop in Maghribi at the international market, listening to Ahmed scold his lazy brother and lament about the Palestinians. You can count to a hundred in forty languages, you can get a room or get a beer or get a joint in twenty-four; you can get by without a word anywhere you go. So why can't you tell her you're leaving? She speaks English, after all. I . . . am . . . leaving . . . you . . . there, wouldn't that feel good? Like the sun in your eyes, like an old sleeper carriage inexorably carrying you away, like a bellyful of grilled lamb and a head full of pipe and the cries of hawkers at midnight on some dirty little side street in a dirty little town whose name you can only pronounce because you've had so much fucking practice. Then you could kiss your friends and kiss her crying eyes and then forget them all to the rock of a ship or the drone of a turboprop or the sound of your bleeding heels walking alone. Wouldn't that be nice?

And, by the way, when are you going to tell her about your vasectomy?

"You're all sunburned!" she cried when she came home, running to fetch ointment from the bathroom. She kissed his reddening nose before applying the cream to his skin with small, deft fingers. "Have you been outside?"

"It's been such a pretty day. I just walked all day."

"You're going to get fired."

She spotted the books on the dining room table; the stack was a foot high, and he'd made no effort to conceal them. "I don't know if I like so much of Miss Isabelle's soul in our house," she said, "I'm liable to get jealous." It was a joke, but he could hear a tinge of possession in her words directed either toward him, or toward a house that a young editor could hardly afford. He didn't try to get her to read the books. She was stubborn, and that was one of the reasons he loved her. They cooked dinner and sat outside and went to bed before ten.

Later, after a few minutes of fumbling, she rolled from his motionless body, her face close to his. "Don't give up on me yet," she said. "Isn't trying supposed to be half the fun?"

He brushed her hair from his face. "That tree—I can hear it." She tilted her head, listening to leaves scrabbling madly at the glass, and he rolled onto his side. "It's distracting, a goddamned nuisance. Maybe we should have it cut down."

"Cut it down with the money you earn."

She rolled over and one of them fell asleep, the other feigned it for a while.

But something awakened her in the middle of the night, and she touched the cold puddle of sheets beside her. She rose from bed as silent as a stalking lioness, and padded across the old wood to come to rest listing against the doorframe of his office, her arms around her herringbone ribs.

"What are you doing?" she asked suddenly, and the quick way his fingers stroked the touchpad of the laptop, the furtive glance and reddening face told her all that she needed to know.

"Distracted, huh. That's a good husband," she told him like she was talking to a dog, and returned to bed.

He looked as though he wanted to say something, but in the end he kept quiet.

You walked today across your town, down streets you know by heart and streets you've stumbled down at three in the morning after ten pints of lager in the rain and still had been unable to get yourself lost . . . you walked these streets today with a small bag across your shoulders, and nothing looked right. Today, nothing looked familiar as you took out a notepad, scribbled a few words, moving between baking cinderblock houses and the smell of tar and grease and horse manure once in a while. That's the thing about smells, though. A Tunisian patisserie, a floating noodle-stall, roasted donkey and cat and rat and all kinds of savory things served up with bread lifted from the concrete by calloused brown fingers. A cigarette taken on the curb of a busy street, sweating. Can you believe you've done all these things? Lying in bed beside her, can you believe that you'll never do them again? Because you can't. Maybe to Paris for a weekend if she gets a raise, or London for a little shopping adventure, because she can't leave her job for six months and even if she could it wouldn't be enough to get her to follow you to Bangladesh. You won't leave her even though last night she was awakened by something (tipped off by that damn tree) and she came stumbling bleary to find you hunched before the screen, and before she could see what you were doing you closed the picture of Aïn Sefra, that Algerian desert outpost where a profound, lonely young woman had lived, where she now rested forever in the sand, and your wife looked at you as though she had caught you staring at some other girl's cunt and you wished suddenly that she had.

Time enough passed for him to read all that Isabelle had ever written, her short stories, her diaries. *The Oblivion Seekers*, pages collected from the mud that had sucked at her poor dead body. He read her thoughts, and he knew her, knew everything about her—she called those she adored *Rouh*, "my beloved." *For those who know the value of and exquisite taste of solitary freedom (for one is only free when alone), the act of leaving is the bravest and most beautiful of all.* He read her thoughts in his own.

The depth of her sense of dispossession stunned him and left him shaking with the kind of empathy that can only be felt towards someone who is you. He wondered about the nature of her spirit that had led her on a life he coveted not because it had been his life once, too, but because she had found her peace.

"Can I crash in your bed tonight? I don't take up much space, and my money's all gone . . . I've come from the desert, oh yeah isn't it sad? Did you make it down to Aïn Sefra? That's where I live. There are palms and olivewood and bats that fly overhead like leather butterflies with teeth. I can show you, if you like. I can show you everything I've ever seen, everything you ever will." The fingers of experience trace circles on your skin; lips taste of the sweetness of hashish and anisette. Then a bell begins to ring somewhere from within the next room in the caravanserai and she tilts her head and climbs from your bed and you hear yourself cry out for her to stay but she's already gone and all that remains is a tickle upon your forehead and an awakening that is funereal.

"Good morning!" she said brightly. "Why did you call me Rouh?"

He pushed himself upright. "When?"

"Just now, when I kissed you."

"Did I?" He felt a smile tug his lips out of shape for an instant. "It's what you say to someone you love."

"Should I say it back? Is that how it works?"

He shook his head.

Saturday once more, crawling shadows purely black on the sidewalks and bitumen. They had made up; they always made up. After all, it had been only a small misunderstanding.

Later, they took their places beneath the honey locust. White lines cut through the stratosphere far above as the tree shrugged, whistled under the force of a confused wind, creaked as though that thick trunk would shatter at any moment. Its leaves were brown, and fell around them. "Do you think it's dying?" she asked him, her voice soft as though afraid the tree might overhear.

"I don't think it knows yet," he said, and she nodded as though she understood.

"Can we go somewhere?"

His face grew suspicious. "What about…" He didn't finish the question, didn't have to.

She finished it. "I guess it's not written, right?"

"Maybe I'm sterile."

She tugged at her coat. "Let's go

somewhere and forget it for a while."

"Where were you thinking?"

"I was hoping you could tell me. Being the expert. But," she added, "It has to be nearby. I only have a week."

A distant backfire, voices drifting across the lawns, and he suddenly started.

"What?" she asked.

"I was just wondering what you'd have looked like covered in dust."

Walking walking too much walking, but you do it because it's what you used to do to get around. One mile, five miles, eighty-six miles once over two weeks through what used to be called Yugoslavia before the rebels rebelled, the ache in your legs is the same. You couldn't abide stillness for very long, not even back then. You tore through China, boiled through Thailand like a venereal disease, hurtled across hammada and piste across moraines through high mountain passes and the passageways of sunken ships bleating bubbles in your face and water warm and tropical against your naked body. Infected infecting always moving even back home in this shit-hole little college town, get some coffee, get a kebab or some babaganoush from your friend Tariq who dreams of the old days even though he's lived in America for forty years—tell me, what chance have you got? Just eat it with your fingers sitting on the

*curb behind the restaurant in the alley, eyes closed.
Wang Faye, Ali Fatu, blaring nameless Indonesian
discord; you thought your ears would bleed after nine
hours in the back of a Jeepney listening to that, so why
are you smiling now at the memory? Shiver from the
cold and it's a relapse of the malaria you can't shake
since the Philippines came through you; that pain in
your side ah don't sweat it . . . it can't be any worse
than the night that followed a pound of raw Burmese
garlic pork. Your prick itches—no, you didn't pick up
anything; you never did the whole sex tour thing. Just
gotta hit the shower. It's been a cold sweaty day sitting
in the lawn chair in the suburbs editing someone else's
manuscript and dreaming with your eyes open. Heels
that have wept your weight in blood ten times over,
lymph nodes that swell sometimes for no good reason,
a head that won't stop thinking and a nose that's far
too sharp. A shower sounds good, but then she comes
home and kisses your mouth and asks about your day
and you tell her you got some really good work done,
a new scene for a book or a start on a new short story
or something like that, and she can't wait to read it
and wonders where you get your ideas and you can
only shrug because you sure as hell can't tell her that
all you think about is leaving, getting lost getting
stranded getting shipwrecked somewhere along the
Barbary Coast while catching a tramp from Miami
to wherever it wants to go as long as it's on the other*

side of the world and sleep can't possibly come, eyelids red like henna, walls Chefchauen blue, drunk tonight not because you want to forget but rather the taste on your tongue takes you back to the Suerta Loca. False hitchhikers faux guides little boys in rags taking your hand smoking Camels and bringing you tea and milk and a picture of someone old baked African air, dust in your mouth but you couldn't close it from smiling. Remember? Smiling stupid bliss in the palmeraie of an ancient Arabic borj that smells of olivewood and heat, smiling because you're home, a place where the Seekers of Oblivion sing and clap their hands, and their dream-voices ring out late into the night; a place where no one is ever missed or expected. Go back she's waiting for you back there waiting for you don't stand her up. You can stretch out in the sand above her, take her sun and fill her grave with tears until she feels them on her dry bones. Pack while she sleeps beside you (under the sad sands of Aïn Sefra) do it now get going because the world waits for no man, especially not for the low man, the married man, but if you won't do it to make me happy or to make me shut up then go the fuck to sleep because I can't think about this anymore

A Cambodian Tale, Part II
(The Sunflower)

Claire first met Erika when their motodops exchanged a knock in heavy Phnom Penh traffic. A Landcruiser swerved, a swaddled figure beneath a cyclo's sunbonnet cursed, the horizon of elephantine buildings tilted drunkenly, and both girls grabbed their respective drivers tightly around the waist as the drivers flashed each other with grins. Foreign surroundings tended to give false feelings of sisterhood, but even though Claire suspected as much, there was something in the way the other girl was laughing that compelled her to risk loosening a hand long enough to give a wave before she spun away down Sisowath Quay.

Several days later, Claire and her friends, a triplet of pale blonde seniors from the University of Vermont, decided to take a public bus down to the coast where there were villages with pretty boys, cheap beer, and nothing else to do but dance and drink and find the kind of frantic, hyper-sentient love that they would never seek out back home. Cambodia had seven roads, all of which radiated from Phnom Penh like the spokes of a junked bike. Their bus took National Road 3 south for five hours, and stopped only when it found water.

The girls took a room at the Blue Door—Claire's friends claimed the beds and left her the rattan couch beneath a barred window. Within minutes, they were in bikinis and flip-flops, examining Claire, who had kept her clothes on, with questioning eyes.

"You all go without me. I'm going to the Sunflower."

"The Sunflower? What's gotten into you, Claire? I thought we were going to go to the beach?" one of the girls asked. "Isn't that what we planned?" This last she addressed to one of the girls flopped on her back beside her, and who now dragged herself upright. The girl yawned and gave a little nod of agreement to her companion. "Let her go, if that's what she wants."

"It's not that, it's just we were supposed to be together!" The first girl turned back to Claire. "Why are you making us fight about this?"

Although Claire was apt to silently absorb criticisms with the merest falter of a distant smile, now she stood. "They're a charity, and I want to see what they're about. Besides," she added, "I'm starving, and they have food."

This seemed to mollify her friend. "Well, get back before six so we can go into town. Jeremy said we should stay in a group, so don't make us miss a night's party. We don't have many left!"

They four of them walked together until they reached the dunes. Here, Claire's friends headed down the sand where the beachside drinking huts clotted at the water's edge like carnival flotsam. Claire, however, stepped into a tide of teenaged boys on slim Honda Citi bikes, baseball caps or green Mao caps shielding their brown faces from the brunt of the afternoon sun. Their chorus was as polite as it was cajoling. "Where you go? I take you! I take you! Madame! Madame!" A pair of them flanked her with their bikes inches from her legs, revving their tiny engines in an odd seduction as they whispered, "Where you wanna go, sister? You want somsing to smoke?"

On the fringe of the pack was a Khmer boy with waves of black hair who hadn't called out anything at all. Up until the moment Claire threw a leg over the passenger seat of his rickety bike and asked him to take her to the Sunflower, he slumped forlornly over the bars, half asleep or pretending to be, but now he yawned theatrically and fingered his cap down to shield himself from the shocked cries of the others before picking a conservative line up the steep dirt road that led into town. He set a considerate pace—Claire could see the needle fluttering at 9 o'clock on the dial over the boy's shoulder; he couldn't have been more than fifteen—but there was dust and vertigo and a sense of flying as the hot wind blew through her hair and against her bare legs. It was hotter here than in Phnom Penh, and what few tourist faces could be found in the village were drinking with her roommates down on the beach. Inland, even a few hundred feet, there were none, and Claire felt like she had come to the edge of the world as the boy turned down alley upon quiet alley, banking into red dirt oxbows beneath masses of heavy pink flowers draped across telegraph poles and crawling along their wires. Dogs slept; children tugged at their fur and grabbed their ears to get them to play.

A few minutes later, the boy pulled to a stop before an impenetrable screen of foliage. Deep green and dense, it cut the lane in half, blocking their way. It was as if even this civilization had run down. The boy pointed ahead. Claire paid him the fare of one dollar, gave him another dollar to see him smile, and then watched him carefully turn his bike and disappear around the bend.

She surveyed the alley. Nothing moved.

After absorbing the stillness for a moment—feeling it in the pit of her stomach and along the insides of her legs, where she had squeezed the boy—Claire pushed through the leaves, and into the Sunflower.

She found herself in a courtyard bounded on all sides by bamboo screens, stucco walls and a sky that had wrung itself of clouds. There were flowers everywhere, and from somewhere nearby came the sound of children playing. Tremendous aromas wafted from the open breezeway that led from the courtyard into the bakery—sugar, coffee, bread, cakes, honey, perfume, incense. For all of these scents of life, however, the place seemed deserted, and Claire, not wishing to intrude too deeply on what was looked increasingly like a private residence, took a seat on a wicker bench before a low, glass table with some magazines on it. Behind her, a palm overflowed its massive cement pot. There were divots in the heavy container, and as Claire absently slipped her finger into one of them, she realized the holes had been gouged by bullets.

Her first of three visitors was a yellow dog that emerged from the house. He moved slyly, feral and circuitous, but licked Claire's hand when she held it before her knees. The dog was followed by a young Khmer girl with a sweet, round face and long black hair who took Claire's order for a cup of coffee and a pastry in careful English colored by an unexpected Australian inflection. The girl arranged a small plate and silverware on the table with a hand that was carved of wood.

Between the magazines on the table, Claire found a laminated sheet that looked like a menu, but when she examined it, she saw that it was not the kind of menu she had been expecting:

SUNFLOWER BAKERY

This is what we did with your December donations of $455.00:

10 mosquito nets. Vitamin supplements for twenty expectant mothers. Antimalarial medicine for five families. School uniforms for three children. School texts for ten children. Purchase of bicycle for student who lived too far from school. Net repair and life jacket for local fisherman. Setting and casting of

broken leg. Vaccinations for two families. Helped build new roof for family house. Amputation surgery with antibiotics, prosthetic, and rehabilitation for one young man.

THANK YOU!!

The yellow dog whimpered and stretched out between her feet, and as he did, Claire realized that someone else was watching her from the arch that led into the house.

"Tam isn't bothering you, is he? Because if he is, I'll have to ask you to leave."

Her voice was low and assured, and although her features were shadowy and indistinct, Claire knew to whom it belonged; she recognized the depth of the voice from the one moment in which she had heard her before, back in the maelstrom of Phnom Penh. The girl obviously recognized her as well, because she came up to her and sat beside her on the wicker lounge as though they were old friends, without surprise or hesitation.

"Welcome to the Sunflower," the girl said, touching her fingertips together before her lightly and bowing her head. "I'm Erika."

There was something very unusual

about the girl from Phnom Penh, Claire thought, even more so than she had mused in the hours following their near-accident. Then, the flashes of silver from the girl's eyebrows and the center of her bottom lip as she had laughed had caught Claire by surprise, as had her hair, which, despite her pale complexion, was almost as dark as a Khmer girl's. Then it had been piled into a carefree twist above the nape of her neck and held there with small, simple clips to reveal the rows of silver hoops that climbed the outside of her ears, and she wore it like that now, long strands falling down either side of her neck and others into her eyes. The angular bones of an ascetic who ate nothing but mangos and fish were revealed by clothes that were airy and loose, and, like a native, her feet were slender and dusty and bare. As Erika settled into the lounge as though it belonged in a tearoom and not before a massive cement flowerpot riddled with bullet holes, Claire decided that what was so unusual about Erika was that Erika was *here*.

"It's lovely, really. Are you responsible for this?"

Erika sighed as Claire indicated the roster of modest accomplishments with a twitch of her head. "Sad, isn't it? These people don't deserve what's happened to them." Her voice was low and

quiet and carried a soft Australian refinement at
the ends of her words that turned each of them
upward and made them float. Claire wished she'd
say something else just to better listen. But Erika
didn't say anything more, so Claire did, mostly
without thinking.

"I'd like to donate something, if I can."

Erika's smile was broad and genuine, but
somehow entirely unsurprised. "Absolutely. That
would be such a great help. I don't mean to sound
ungrateful, but I'm afraid I'm going to have to
beg you for every cent you've got." She pulled
a strand of hair from the corner of her mouth
and gave a little laugh in a manner that Claire
thought mixed frustration, hope, exhaustion
and ultimately, defeat, in equal measure. Even
as Erika slumped a little lower beside Claire,
Claire's thoughts were crystallizing, her eyes
on December's Accomplishments. The Khmer
girl with the sweet face and the wooden hand
was watching from an alcove as Claire breathed
air that smelled like a dusty summer field, all
fireweed and sky. Tam pricked his ears to listen.

"I'm going to give you five hundred and
thirty dollars."

Erika blinked twice as though there
were a speck in one of her wide, dark eyes, and
then wrapped Claire in a hug tight enough to

still both of their breaths. Claire was shocked by the momentary touch of cool metal as Erika kissed the side of her neck before pulling back and examining Claire at arm's length and shaking her head. "I thought you looked like a heroine when we mixed it up in Phnom Penh. A real girl of action."

"Hemingway once said, 'never confuse action with motion.'" Heat rose into her cheeks and she examined her hands and spoke to them instead of Erika. "I read the things you're trying to do. It's amazing, *you're* amazing, and I want to help."

"Are you sure you'll have enough left over? To get home, and all that?"

"I don't know that I even want to." Claire giggled. "But I'll get my dad to wire some when I get back to Phnom Penh in a few days. He's a dentist, and he said that I should 'for God's sake take whatever I need to keep me safe in that horrible country.'" She grinned with a sense of sudden camaraderie. "It's what we need, right?"

"You've no idea." Erika stroked Tam behind the ears. "Listen: I have to take care of a few things around here before I close, but what are you doing later?"

Claire put her hand on Tam's head beside Erika's, and Tam looked smug, and Claire thought of her friends, and shrugged. "Nothing."

"In that case, hang out for a while?"

Claire made two small fists and then sighed. "I'm supposed to meet some people and go to a club. It'll be awful, but it would be immoral to stand them up. I'm going to hate every second of it. I'd feel a lot better if I stayed here."

Erika pursed her lips. "'What is moral is what you feel good after.' The big EH again." As Claire's mouth fell open with unabashed delight, Erika stood, and extended her hand. "I guess I'll see you around, Claire."

"I'll stay, I'll stay!"

As she waited for Erika, Claire selected a magazine but was unable to concentrate. Mosquitoes hummed in her ears, not quite daring to land, and geckos clung to vines and walls, feasting on the mosquitoes. A pair of scruffy travelers broached the greenery, two men asking the Khmer girl for coffee and Erika. They got their coffee but not Erika, and Claire was unreasonably happy when they left.

Everything grew still. Voices came from upstairs rooms of the house, and for a while, Claire clearly heard Erika patiently intoning what sounded like a grocery list—banana, ba*na*na; mango, *man*go; porridge, *por*ridge. Then came another voice muttering. Eventually, the voices merged, and then abruptly stopped, and were soon followed by the sound of water running. Twenty minutes later, Erika emerged. Colorful sandals adorned her feet, her hair was damp, and she had changed her shirt and put on a shadow of lipstick. Claire wished that she'd had the time to do the same, and she told Erika this as she led them around the side of the house.

Erika looked surprised. "I only did it to keep up with you."

Claire didn't know what to say, and Erika laughed. "I've been baking all day. It was starting to show."

The bike was 250 cubic centimeters of dubious parentage, tall on its shocks and knobby tires, unsteady as a drunk unless it was throwing itself into turns. Erika steadied it for Claire, then handed her a pair of sunglasses.

"There's nothing to it—just grab me and don't let go."

Erika kicked the machine to life and they burst from within the shrubbery of the bakery like escaping spies. She held the twist-grip tight against its stop and pushed the bike until it screamed beneath them, tearing up the dirt streets and kicking gravel on every curve. Motodops and their fares—young boys going to evening English lessons, a triplet of girls riding sidesaddle coming from the market, a teen holding a pair of dead geese by the neck in each hand so that their bodies flapped like bloody white balloons—watched enviously as they tore past.

To her surprise, Claire found that she wasn't frightened in the least. The sun was falling, and the unfolding tableau was washed with pale, warm colors. It was like flying into an old, scratched photograph, and Claire locked her hands around Erika's hips and pressed her face against the bones of her back as the Cambodian scenery fled past.

"You drive like we're being chased!"

The front tire caught a brick and the bike briefly lost touch with the ground. Claire gasped. Erika laughed.

"Don't you know we are?"

Chez Claudia was a collection of toadstools sprouting from the top of a bald headland overlooking the sea, and it was here, after parking their bike at the foot of the hill, that Erika led Claire, arms linked tightly against the night. During the course of the ten-minute climb, Erika filled Claire in about Claudia, who was an expatriate Frenchwoman who had lived here for twenty years. She rented out some of the bungalows when it suited her, took her friends diving off Koh Thmei and the surrounding islands that were scattered like hazy visions across the blue water, and occasionally cooked for her most favored friends.

"One of the benefits of being a long-timer," Erika told Claire as they approached the hard, boyish woman in her early fifties waiting at the head of the final flight of wooden stairs. Claudia gave Erika a hug, and shook Claire's hand and bowed, before leading them to their table. It was the only one on a balcony made of thick timbers cantilevered over the swells two hundred feet below. The atmosphere was freighted with flowers—bougainvillea and jasmine—and salt.

"What do we do?" Claire asked. There didn't seem to be any menus or organized service at all.

Erika waved as though it didn't matter. "She'll give us whatever she wants to make, and I promise you'll love it."

A boy brought them wine. The girls toasted without articulating their toast.

"It's so beautiful here," Claire said, glancing at the scenery and the ocean far below. "How did you end up in this place? How did you know you could do this?"

Erika brushed some hair from her face.

"When I came here a few years ago, I was a real mess. I was working in this record shop back home, watching all my old friends graduate from university, get jobs, get lives. It was depressing, not because I wanted to be like them, but because it made me realize how much I *didn't*."

Claire nodded quickly. These weren't the emotions of a stranger; they might well have been her own, and she motioned for Erika to continue.

"One year, someone asked me to come with him on a two-week vacation here, and I quit work that day," Erika said.

"How long ago was that?"

"Four years next month. When I got here, I went around and saw what people were doing to help, and when I saw how much I could do, to help build something I could never build in Melbourne, I told my friend that I was staying. He thought I was crazy, but these have been the best years of my life, without a doubt." Erika took a sip of the wine, but her eyes never left Claire's. "Sometimes people with special skills come through. For instance, you wouldn't have recognized poor Tam last month. He'd gotten into a scrap with another dog, and had his throat ripped open. Not immediately fatal, but getting that way—things don't heal here. We didn't have money to patch him up; imagine letting a little kid die because we used the money to fix up our stray. A few days later, a girl came to the bakery. I talked with her for a little while, not about anything, really, just the way I talked with you. And she took one look at Tam and said she was a veterinarian. She bought antiseptic, bandages, and patched him up." Erika shook her head as though had she not witnessed it, the story would strain her credulity. "People want to help. They *want* to."

"People want to help you," Claire added.

Erika put her wine glass down. "Mothers here get beri beri—B1 tablets are all they need to make the difference between a healthy life and paralysis." Erika sighed. "There is no insurance, there is no welfare, there is no health care system. There's just us." She let the words sink like stones through dark water, let Claire feel their weight.

"What about the non-governmental organizations? Don't they do anything?"

Erika nodded very quickly, but her eyes flashed. "Sure they do. They do plenty. Administrative costs take up 70 percent of your average NGO's funds. And they have very specific criteria that must be met before they even think about helping. We use 100 percent of our money to help those Khmers who fall through the cracks."

Erika seemed to run out of air then, and slipped into a sullen silence. There was nothing to add, so Claire gave her space, and eventually the last of the twilight bled away from the horizon and the warmth of the night and the stars hanging low subdued her indignity, if only for a while. Erika brought her chair around to Claire's side of the table and they sat side by side, sharing a bowl of ice cream and whispering so Claudia, leaning against the rail in the adjacent hut smoking a cigarette, couldn't overhear. They talked for hours not as travelers in faraway places do, telling each other where they had been, but as sojourners—only interested in those things that were in the now and a little further ahead than that.

"Do you realize, Claire, that in most of these places, it's us girls who are in charge?" It sounded like a question so often pondered that it had long since ceased to be a question, but Claire made a questioning noise anyway. "The bloody men—the boys, I should say—run around Snookyville or in the markets of Phnom Penh like they're commandos or something. It's like coming across a pair of Cambodian tourists lurking about the food court in the Queen Victoria Building in downtown Sydney, pretending it's exotic and dangerous while mums push their prams up and down the aisles of David Jones." She trailed away in bubbles of laughter, and Claire, thankful her earlier darker mood seemed long forgotten, couldn't stop smiling. Erika grabbed her hand as it lay palm-up on her leg between them, and squeezed it hard in a gesture of solidarity and friendship.

"Equality is shit. I tell you, Claire, we're the evolution."

Specks of light cut across invisible swells far out to sea, boats returning to port, as Erika spoke again, softer still. "When I said I needed every cent you had, that's exactly what you gave me, isn't it." The statement wasn't a question at all, and Claire couldn't meet her eyes. The admission seemed like one of weakness, and she didn't want Erika to see it. She needn't have worried.

"I have an idea," Erika said, suddenly sleepy, her chin propped by her hand. "Say yes and I'll be your friend for life."

"Yes."

Erika pulled Claire to her feet. "Heroine, like I said."

Cambodian mornings, especially those by the sea, are some of the most amazing in the world.

In the mist rising from the jungle, the smoke from fires lit by women and watchmen, and the cries of monkeys, that Cambodian morning sun was the color of the robes of the monks burning beneath it; more than that, it was a hole leading to the gallery in which the robes were made.

It was this sort of morning that found Claire waiting anxiously on the stoop of her bungalow, where she had taken residence an hour before, unable to sleep. Her friends—tousled, muttering and suspicious—had returned home not long after, but they ignored the sunrise in order to better effect a trio of filthy glances, and filled the room with their snores and narcoleptic gasps minutes later. Claire found a quieter spot to sit a little away from the bungalow and waited.

She heard the engine and saw the plume of red dust well before the bike crested the hill. Standing on the pegs with equestrian grace, posting with her legs and arms to absorb the wildly bucking machine beneath her, Erika gunned down the rutted slope, waking motodops whose bare brown feet were just visible beneath the flowers as they slept in the bushes beside their own frail and rusting steeds. They peered at her as she locked the back tire and skidded up to the bungalow. The bike steamed and snorted as Claire threw her leg over its back.

Erika twisted around in the saddle. Her hair was pulled into a ponytail, and her dark eyes were narrowed. "Hold on to this case, Claire. It's vital nothing happens to it."

Claire fingered the tattered leather case. It was light, like most of its substance had decayed and was long gone. "What's in it?"

"Top secret papers. We have to get it to my girl in the jungle, or you don't want to know what will happen to her."

"How much time has she got?"

"A few hours, at best."

"Will it be a dangerous mission?" Claire whispered.

"Absolutely. The road is filled with all manner of nasties; where do you think you are? This isn't Vermont—are you up for it?"

"Absolutely."

Monkeys were brown shrieks that leapt from tree to tree keeping pace as the old bike flew along the jungle track. Soon, the mangroves gave way to teak, and they skirted puddles that could have swallowed trucks and probably had, fallen trees, cows and chickens and little laughing girls who called out to them as they passed, and to whom Erika always cried Khmer greetings, which made them laugh all the more. Water buffalo splashed in murky ponds, their hocks coated with duckweed, their broad backs tight over their bones and glistening almost blue, their horns swept back and sage. They watched with placid faces as the girls careened through rivulets of water washing the track, Erika laughing, Claire tucked tightly against her back to duck the sheets of warm spray. Erika's hair tickled Claire's nose, strands of it were in her mouth, and as they wound deeper into the misty hills, farther away from everything she had ever known about herself or her world, Claire knew there would be many things she would forget before this.

Erika killed the bike beside a tidy shack built on stilts above a cracked rice paddy. As she held it for Claire so that she could step down, a group of shirtless boys and girls boiled out from the lower level of the stilt-house, brown and glistening and howling with delight. Claire lifted the leather case above her head as if she were wading into deep water, but Erika squatted between the children and was promptly swallowed up in flailing brown arms. When she stood, she was holding one of the girls on her hip.

Claire laughed. "You'd make a great mother."

"Would I?" Erika asked, bouncing the little girl higher, and then kissing her on a very round cheek. "Let's adopt her. We'll live together in a hut by the ocean and raise her as our own."

Claire tilted her head, and Erika burst into laughter just as a man in his forties wearing tattered Khaki pants and a *krahma* around his head limped out of the house. He approached the girls, maneuvering ably on legs that were both made of wood. Erika set the little girl down and bowed before him. He pulled the red and white checked cloth down to reveal a skeletal, radiant face.

"Tuon, this is my good friend Claire."

Tuon introduced himself carefully, the beginnings of an Australian accent of which Claire could guess the origins refining his words. She bowed, and Tuon's hands were like galled sticks pulled from mud as they tented before his chest, dipped once and then parted.

Erika touched Claire's shoulder to lift her gaze from the ground, and began speaking rapidly. "Tuon bought this land six years ago as a place where he could grow rice and vegetables and provide a place to raise his children. He took possession of it during the dry season. When the rains came, the ground softened, and where for five months there had been safe passage, he sank onto a mine that lay a centimeter beneath the center of the path that led from the house to the paddy behind it." She pointed along it, and Claire saw the tin and wood fort at its end, where the children liked to play. "Yeah. His kids ran up and down that path a hundred times a day, and his wife carried washing there, too. The awful thing was the mine was in really bad nick."

Claire raised her eyebrows, and Erika added patiently, "The mine was rusted out, so it mangled his legs, but didn't remove them completely. It happens all the time."

Claire still didn't understand why it was better to have your legs blown off than have them broken or cut up. After all, cuts and breaks healed; gone was gone. In this country, she was getting a sense of that word, enough at least to not take it lightly. "Why is *that* the awful thing?"

"Things around here don't heal. Infections, fractures, shrapnel wounds—they fester and weep. Often gangrene sets in and settles matters, but many times a strange balance forms, and the wound never gets any worse, but nor does it get any better. Tuon was like that. He lay destitute on the floor of this house as it fell apart around him, a beggar dependent even for that upon his children, while his wife worked in a granary in Poipet. We got the money up to get his feet removed and to install the very basic but functional wooden ones you can see on him now.

It changed his life, and ours as well."

All throughout Erika's explanation, Tuon was nodding, as though he understood it, or had heard it many times before and was as familiar with its substance as the toddlers of evangelists were familiar with the mythologies of their parents. The children, however, were familiar with more pressing issues, and they tugged at Claire's hands, trying to show her childish things—a swollen black beetle gnashing the shears of its jaws, a doll made of sticks and scraps of fabric. Claire nodded seriously at each item, but didn't touch either of them.

"Tuon," Erika said, glancing at Claire, who still held tightly to the attaché case. "It's important that my friend get this to your wife."

Tuon led the girls beneath the house, where a smiling woman greeted Erika. Erika introduced Claire to Mliss as Tuon repaired to his tattered brown hammock, within whose folds he vanished like an insect in a cocoon.

Erika nodded at Claire. She held out the case. Mliss took it from her carefully, and Claire clapped her hands together and stepped behind Erika. She peered anxiously over Erika's shoulder as Mliss pulled out a sheaf of yellowed papers filled with complicated diagrams. Behind her, Tuon's cocoon swelled and deflated in rhythm to his soft snores. The children tugged on her hands, both of them now free and dangling loosely at her sides. She ignored them and held her breath as Mliss flipped through the thick sheaf of pages.

The diagrams were familiar somehow, and Claire sidled forward to see. Erika watched her face as Claire studied the curves, the patterns, the templates. . . . She burst out into laughter and finally let the children drag her down to their playhouse beside the dried-up paddy. Erika sat on the ground with Mliss and went through the sewing patterns with her, their heads close together and their voices low. What seemed like not more than a minute later, Erika and Mliss were on their feet and saying goodbye. The children looked stricken.

"This was the mission?" Claire asked Erika as they made their way back to the bike. "We just drove two hours to give her sewing patterns?"

"Yup. She's been looking forward to them for weeks." Erika stared into the cracks in the dry ground. She didn't seem to want to leave them. The children were beginning to cluster again, and Erika put her hand down and took hold of a little boy who was readying to press his palm against the hot muffler to test himself against it.

"Sometimes I can't do this alone, you know?"

"What about the Khmers you have working at the shop? You're building the country, in a way. You must have help."

"Bothdara and Chieang and Savorn came to work with us after they were patched up. Did you know Bothdara is studying to be a chef? I'll ask him to make you some *samlau m'choo* when we get back. Sour fish soup. He won't mind a bit."

"But?"

"But it isn't the same as having someone I can *talk* to. As much as I love them and I think they love me, there is always that separation between the colonizers and the natives." She sighed. "There are people who come and go, but for the most part, I'm on my own for long periods of time. And as nice as the Khmers are, being alone in a place like this can be rough. You can feel it, can't you. Like sitting on a tire swing over a bloody great drop, back and forth, back and forth." She swept the hair from her forehead. Its darkness made the pallor of her skin all the more apparent, and the silver ring, emerging from the fullness of her bottom lip, flashed in the sun. "Maybe you can't feel it, I don't know." Erika shrugged. "Are you disappointed?"

At that moment, Claire had an odd thought, one she would replay in her head much later many times but most often when nights turned freezing and she was out walking alone. Above Erika, the sun flamed the palms on the horizon, her bike, her shoulders, her feet turned inward like those of a child, slender and dusty. The sun burned these things into her eyes, and Claire thought: *No one in the world knows where I am, but you.*

The ride out had been on the back of a rush she had never before felt, but it was on the ride back that Claire decided to stay.

When she told her girlfriends she wouldn't be going home with them, their reaction was as she had expected.

"You've sold your ticket? What's gotten into you, Claire? What about school? You've got three years under your belt! You can't just *stay!*"

Claire whirled on the girl who had said this, a girl with pale blue eyes and heavy, pink shoulders. "Tell me what I'm going to do with a degree in English? Undergrad from U of Vermont? I'll be qualified to make burgers or baby sit or—or sell records! Meaningless! I don't want to be meaningless."

"Sell records? What are you talking about? No one even listens to records anymore! And no one told you to pick English, Claire." She crossed her arms over her stomach as though trying to hide it. "Don't you want to get a good job, a husband? Start a family?" She rubbed her stomach. "God I'm starving."

"You have no right to say that here! And people do listen to records! What do you think the D.J.'s are spinning at the clubs where you get pickled every night? CDs?"

The girl with the heavy pink shoulders lowered them and shook her head. Her friend stepped in.

"Did you meet someone? Is that it?"

"No! I mean, yes, but not like that. You wouldn't get it."

"We've been friends for six semesters!"

Claire thrust back against the lounge. "I've been looking for something for a long time. Okay? Just because I didn't tell *you* doesn't mean it wasn't there." Claire sighed. "But I think it might be here. It feels right, right here. Better than anything I've ever felt with anyone."

"So you did meet someone. Way to treat your boyfriend, Claire."

"A half-dozen dates hardly qualifies him as my boyfriend. James Michener once said—"

"Oh, can the book-talk, would you? You don't know James Michener, whoever he is. You're always doing that, talking like they're your friends."

Claire bit her lip and continued, a little more slowly, a little surer of herself. "James Michener said once, after he almost died: 'I don't know if I can be a great man, but I am determined to live as if I am.'"

"So you want to be a great man, do you?" There was laughter all around, and Claire knew she was through explaining herself. There was one person who understood her, and that was enough.

The next morning, she moved out of the Blue Door and into Erika's bungalow at the far end of town.

Claire would remember those few days that followed her decision to abandon the country of her birth as some of the sweetest she would ever know. Mornings, she helped Erika in the bakery, kneading dough and dusting sugar over soft, golden pastries, which they sold to hotels in Sihanoukville, and to the small but steady trickle of foreigners who made it this far. Many of these scruffy young men were expatriates who brought in all manner of goods for Erika—crates of soap or toothbrushes, old clothes, books to practice English, old eyeglasses—which she distributed throughout the town. Claire took over the English classes, although class was too grand a term; there were two students, but they were eager and kind-faced, and Claire loved hearing them work difficult words over and over until they got them just right. She loved looking up unexpectedly to find Erika in the doorway gazing absently at her as she guided the hands of her students to draw neat alphabets. She loved it when Tam put his head in her lap while Erika tidied up the kitchen between customers, and closed up the shutters when the night settled around them, heavy with moisture and dark Cambodian fragrances.

In this country filled with shadows, frequent power outages, and leaves as large as umbrellas, Erika took Claire to her favorite haunts, introducing her as her sister in some places, in others as "the girl who saved my life." They walked together along miles of moonlit sand, and once swam from Victory to Occheutal and Serendipity Beach listening to old Van Morrison on the air from the bungalows beneath the headland. They drank tea and coffee and beer and wine, ate fish and shrimp and mangoes that made their lips taste sweet when they brushed against each other to whisper jokes or ideas for the future or when they said goodnight. They slept in the same bed like sisters.

There was no television, no phone, and

Claire forgot her worries at home, the professors she had hated as they pontificated about the importance of Flaubert but had never been in a place like this to see what was really important. She forgot her friends, who had left the Blue Door a few days after she had moved out. She got her dad to send more money, almost two thousand dollars, but then told him she wouldn't be coming back after all.

Another few weeks passed, and then she forgot him too.

For Claire, time sputtered and then stalled somewhere along the 11th parallel. It didn't start grinding forward again with its painful familiarity until some time later, as the girls lay together in bed.

The mosquito net billowed and sighed above them. Claire's legs were rubbery from another endless evening, bobbing far offshore with Erika, floating for hours on their backs and staring at the stars. Now, the air was coming off the ocean in salty waves, filling Claire's lungs and clearing the doubts in her head.

"Have you decided what you want to do with my dad's money?" Claire asked the darkness above them. Claire had been drawing a little money from the bakery—it cost a few dollars a day to live here—and so the sum was largely untouched, the greenbacks stuffed into a sock behind the frame of Claire's pack. Erika rolled onto her side, her face inches from Claire's, so that Claire could smell the sea on her skin. "'Orphaned elders.'"

"What're they?" Claire asked. *Is my voice shaking?*

"Old people whose kids—the social security of the third world—have been murdered by the KR, or maimed or killed by mines, or disease, or starvation, or . . . you get the idea. Before you came, we were trying to get funding to build a place just for them." Erika paused. "Have you noticed anything about Khmers, not just here, but all over the country? Unlike in Thailand or Viet Nam, what do you rarely see?"

Claire thought for a moment, and then it hit her. "Gray hair," she said softly, and Erika made a small noise as though she were proud. "You don't see Cambodians with gray hair. God, I've been here for a month now and I never realized that before." Suddenly the room gave a twirl. "You can get it done with the money my dad sent?"

"Yes we can."

They were quiet for a while, thinking on different things, until Claire mustered herself again. "I love being here."

"I love you here."

"I've never been so content as when I'm with you. I've never been this happy." She made a small sound. "I've never been happy."

"And I can't believe how lucky I am that you stayed on to help us."

Claire laughed, relieved. "Who is this 'us' you keep mentioning? I've only ever seen you!"

"Russel."

Claire crinkled her nose and gave a sideways twitch with her head, as though a hair had fallen into her eye.

Erika went on. "My boyfriend. He's driving in from Thailand next week. Been gone for six months. *Decompressing*, he says." She said the word snidely, but with obvious affection. "I told you the night we met—he was the one who brought me out here in the first place. When I wasn't leaving, he said he'd stay here as well, remember? *Couldn't bear to leave me*, he said." She took Claire's hand and squeezed it. "I can't wait for you to meet him. After so long, *I* can't wait to meet him."

Claire tried to pull her hand from Erika's to brush the hair from her face, which still seemed to be hurting her and blurring her vision, but Erika held tightly to her. Claire gave up and their hands lay atop one another in the concavity of her bare stomach like fish. "We'll be able to get so much more done with some real help." There was no doubt about it now; Claire's voice was shaking.

Erika's breath carried the scent of the tropical flowers that grew outside their windows. "And after, think of it—maybe a little schoolhouse, or a communal plot of land where a couple of families can farm. What would we do without you?" She laughed, and added, "If only your dad knew what we were doing with his money, he might even be proud."

"You don't know my dad," Claire said.

Erika fell asleep but Claire stayed awake, savoring the warmth of the night. The wind often blew from the ocean here after dark, and it came up now, rocking the empty hammocks beneath the palms and filling their bedroom with the sound of gentle water. She listened to Erika breathe until it was time to go.

Silently, Claire left her bed and slipped her things into her backpack—all but the sock of money, which she left behind. Outside, Claire let her eyes roam over the bungalow, the yard filled with flowers, and then she turned her back to them. On the beach, beneath the hole that led to the gallery of the robes, barefoot in the smoke from a hundred fires, there was nothing but flat black water and broken shells at the high water line.

Acknowledgements

My most heartfelt thank you:

To Todd Simmons, for taking publishing back to its roots, and for believing in me and in this small book. Whatever you do in life, I'll always be honored to stand beside you.

To my parents, Agnes and Tibor Rozgonyi, for giving me a most amazing childhood filled with adventure and stability, love and inspiration, with plenty of room left over for daydreaming, which is what I do best.

To all the amazing folks at Wolverine Farm Publishing and Matter Journal who supported me and accepted me as one of their own, and whom I count most emphatically among those in my life, both past and present, who have made me what I am. To Sue Ring deRosset and Evan P Schneider especially, who in addition to these things, were my eyes when my own were exhausted.

To Elizabeth J. Gilbert, for being a brilliant writer and human being in general, and for always keeping me good company.

Finally, although this book is a work of fiction, all fiction is fact when we get right down to it, and so I want to thank the people I have been fortunate enough to meet on my travels—Chinese soldiers whose hospitality stunned me; the beautiful saviors of the provinces of Cambodia; the Lion who still stalks his prey amid the ruined alleys of Fez; and all the rest I only glimpsed from the corners of my eyes but who never again left my head. In showing me their homes and lives, they taught me more things than I could ever write down, but none more important than this: Pretty much all the people in the world want to meet you. Don't let anyone scare you into believing otherwise. Get out there and say hello to as many of them as you can while you're here—there is no better thing you can do.

So thanks for reading, but now it's time to stick this in your pocket, take up your pack, and hit it. The next time we meet, it had better be on the road.

DR
Fort Collins, Colorado
November 2005

This book is set in Janson, a typeface inspired by Hungarian punchcutter M. Kis in 1685. This version of Janson text is the most authentic digital version of the original Kis types. Layout and design by Todd Simmons. Printed on KnightKote Matte® recycled paper using elemental chlorine-free pulps in acid-free and chlorine-free manufacturing conditions, exceeding archival standards.

Travel Mate Contest

Think of somewhere in the world you've always wanted to see, someplace exciting and adventurous and unforgettable. Got it? Now, in 150 words or less and on a separate piece of paper, tell David where in the world you want to go, and why. If you're the lucky winner, he'll plan his next adventure there, and take you along for the ride!

Grand Prize is a 10-day, all-expense paid adventure. Entries must NOT contain entrant's name, except on the form on the opposite page. Entries must be typed, and attached to the opposite page. Yes, we are asking you to cut out the last page of this book, which is your original entry form. Don't lose it, or mangle it too much while cutting, as it must be included with your submission. Contest open from 29 April 2006 until 15 February 2007. Winner will be picked by a combination of merit and anonymous drawing on or about 21 February 2007. Trip must be taken within one calendar year of that date. Must be 18 or older and a U.S. citizen to participate.

Visit www.wolverinefarmpublishing.org or www.davidrozgonyi.com for complete official rules, dates and contest restrictions.